Ruthless Ambition

A.N. Hayes

Duke and I Publishing

ISBN-13: 978-0-9916080-0-3
ISBN-10: 0-991-60800-3

Dedicated to my family, by blood, by marriage or by love. Thank you for your constancy and support.

one

"She did it again," Nora said, softly, under her breath. Nora should not have been surprised, but somehow she never remembered the full frustration until it happened again. She and her mother were supposed to be eating lunch right now. But instead, Nora was sitting at the table, waiting for her to show up. Again. So far, she was twenty minutes late but could be ten or more if she ran true to form. The server sighed, as he looked her way. She was holding up a precious lunchtime table that he could be half way to turning over if her mother had been there on time. This was their monthly lunch date at Paulette's, a popular restaurant in midtown Memphis. Nora loved her mother and the food was delicious, but she wondered if it was worth it. Laura Anderson would be a generous tipper, but the server didn't know that yet. It was a waste of energy to get so annoyed since she was always late. And of course as soon as she arrived, Nora would swallow down her frustration and not let it ruin their time together. She did, however, always point it out to her mother.

"Are you ready to order or are you still waiting?" The server asked.

"I'll just wait a few more minutes. Sorry." She answered. He nodded back to her, trying to affect the patience of Job. Nora sipped her iced tea and read over the menu for the third time, trying to look serious instead of the loiterer she was. She stole a quick glance around the room. Everyone was talking and eating.

"I can't believe she said that. You should tell her. She has a right to know, and it would serve her right to find out," said a lady sitting at the table next to her. Nora didn't want to hear about the tragedies of an unknown relationship. Her stomach growled audibly as she spotted the food served to the lady's table. Okay, enough. She flagged the server to order for them both. He stopped in mid stride, his attention captured by a cacophony of movement and sound from the back of the restaurant. The sounds grew louder and more strained until the pop sound drew silence. After a few seconds of realization verses denial, the noise became deafening. People shouted and knocked over chairs to get to the front, away from the sound of gunfire. Nora's first thought was of her mother, since she normally came in through the rear

5

entrance. She jumped up and fought her way against the crowd of hysterical old ladies. No one tried to stop her as she ran down the now deserted back hallway. It was short and the half-windowed door at the end was closed all but three or four inches. Voices were yelling outside, but not like the panic inside. These were the voices of an angry man and a scared, pleading man. At the sound of those voices she stopped her momentum and did not push open the door. She looked out the window, still searching for her mother, but instead saw a car screech to a halt in the alley. A furious black man stopped his tirade. He leveled his gun at the younger black man sitting on the ground holding his middle, and fired. In a split second the younger man went from sitting to lying flat on his back. Nora looked for his face but there wasn't one recognizable. She felt such an intense wave of fear that she couldn't move. She tried to scream but no sound came out. She wanted to turn and run but her arms and legs refused. Her eyes were the only responsive parts. They instinctively looked to the source of the last shot. They met with two legs and a hand holding a gun, but the awning over the door was blocking the head and neck of the shooter. The man moved toward her and she could not breathe, much less defend herself. Nora did not want to see his face and yet could not stop her eyes from drifting up. From the new angle she could see him clearly as he looked up and saw her. The driver honked the horn and the shooter looked another second before turning away to get in the car. The tires squealed down the road as she heard sirens in the background. She started breathing again, gasping really. The eyes of the shooter were etched into her brain but little else was. Then her rough breaths turned into sobs. Nora was shaking and crying, unable to stop either. Several minutes went by before she thought of her mother again.

Obviously Laura Anderson had missed the fight and the murder. They were in the heart of Memphis, which made it easy for the police to arrive quickly. Then an ambulance drove up. Although Nora was a nurse, it never occurred to her to try and save the man with no face. Maybe it was revulsion, maybe just the futility of the act, but she felt ashamed nevertheless. Head and facial shootings are not always fatal, but she found it impossible to believe that was the case here. She drifted back into the main dining room and dropped into her seat. The police were asking everyone to stay inside so the room was filled with anxious people. Noticing her state of near hysteria, people started asking Nora questions to which she reflexively muttered responses. Now exactly why she answered every question posed to her is somewhat a mystery and possibly attributed to shock. She should have waited and only answered the police questioning. But since she was unable to apply the simplest judgment she made a mistake that would be the root of all her problems to follow.

"Nora! What happened, are you hurt?" Her mother asked, as she rushed to the table.

"I'm fine, just a little upset," she answered, sniffling but under control. Laura abruptly broke into tears of relief. Nora gave her a minute to recover,

"Where were you? I was afraid you were the one who had been shot," Nora asked.

"I was about to turn into the alley and park in the back lot, but I saw some men pushing and shouting at each other so I decided to circle around the block," her mother said. By the time she got around one of what she considerers a block, five minutes had passed and there were police cars on their way to the scene. Of course, if the police were driving down the street with their sirens on, her mother would come to a complete stop for as long as it took for every police car to go by. Then she had to park in an unfamiliar lot because the back lot was now filled with emergency vehicles. And finally she had to convince the police to let her in the building since they were beginning to let some people out. It was during this struggle that she heard her daughter's name and description being given to reporters by the restaurant staff and patrons. These accounts made her all the more panicked, and determined to get in. She punctuated her story by succumbing to more tears. Nora calmed and reassured her until it was her turn to be interviewed.

Laura Anderson heard the facts unfold as the police questioned her daughter. She became more focused and less upset, beginning to see the danger in the situation before Nora did. Her shock had numbed her to the possibilities. Laura also had the knowledge that the press had too many details and were broadcasting them irresponsibly as they spoke. She insisted the police talk to the reporters and demanded they stop the broadcast. A weak attempt was made, but the police knew it would be impossible and really blamed Nora for talking in the first place. Nora couldn't defend herself or even tell them exactly what she said because the truth was she didn't remember for sure. Even though she had been frightened many other times in her life, she had only reacted as she had today one other time. And that night Nora had not been able to move or scream, even though she tried desperately to do so. The extreme fear was her only excuse.

Laura saw Nora's fear and took control, calling her second daughter, Helen, who would pick up Nora's car from the restaurant then go to her house to pack some clothes. Nora would need clothes because Laura also determined Nora must stay at her parent's home.

Her father was angry. He had always been overprotective but this sent him to a whole new level. Laura and Nora were lectured on their choice of dining establishments, even though it happened to be one of his favorite places to eat. Then of course, they both agreed that she was foolish for running toward gunshots rather than away from them. Certainly she could see their wisdom but it had not been a conscious decision. Then they started the familiar lecture on thinking before acting. That did it. Nora had to leave.

"Dad, I appreciate your concern and I'm sorry you are so worried, but I'm fine. I can't run home every time something scary happens," she said.

"Of course you can. What better time is there to come home? You know I can keep you safe here, or anywhere," he argued. There was no doubt that was true. Sam Anderson owned a security company. But any eyes on her would be his eyes. It took a long time to get out from under the umbrella of Sam's world, but she did. Nora would not give up that autonomy easily, and certainly not for something like this, which was likely over.

"I know you can. And I'll come to you if I need that. But you should understand why I can't let fear dictate my decisions. I've worked hard to build this life; I won't just abandon it," she said.

"Nora, don't be so dramatic. No one says you have to give up your life, just take a break until this blows over. Your mother will be in a state if you go home alone," he said.

"I won't go home. I plan to spend the night with Stephan and Monica Ross," she said. She and Monica had been friends since high school. She and her husband were Nora's closest friends. She knew they would let her stay and their company would go a long way to making things feel normal again.

"What? You know I love Monica like a daughter and Stephan is a good man but why would you go to them over staying here with us?" He asked. "Nora, you're tired and in shock. This isn't the best time to rebel against your parents. I'm not saying you should move back home, just spend the night." He made sense on some level but she knew the power of Sam's persuasiveness. It would start as just one night, then two, then the next thing she knew a moving truck has brought the contents of her house to his. No, rational or not, she wouldn't go back home.

It was telling that Sam hadn't mentioned her boyfriend, Allen. He was out of town on business, but dad didn't know that. She really wished he were here. His strength and quiet disposition made her feel calm and helped her to think clearly. Also, she could have stayed with him, but wouldn't have told her father. It wasn't that he didn't like Allen; he didn't know him. That was a big part of the problem. She hadn't introduced them. They had only been dating a few months and her father was not the casual type. Any introduction would have been loaded. He would have given Allen the full court press, assuming she might chose him to marry. Then after making everyone feel awkward, Sam would have done a full background check on him. It's not that she was worried about what he would find, but just that she didn't want someone's civil liberties violated because he chose to date her. Since she hadn't made Allen walk the family gauntlet, Sam assumed he was inconsequential. There may have been some truth to that, but she was just dating the guy. She wasn't ready to declare him a keeper or throw him away. Couldn't they just give it some time, to see where it goes?

But even if the family had vetted him, her father would not have welcomed any competition in the "taking care of Nora" department. She didn't expect to hear from Allen until later in the evening and decided not to call because she really didn't want to talk now. It was unlikely he would see or hear anything about the incident on the news since he was in Houston.

"Dad, they have no connection to what has happened. No one will look for me there, especially not reporters. It shouldn't take them long to find my house and then to figure out your connection next. I don't need any more exposure," she said. Nora didn't want to hurt his feelings but she wasn't staying. This argument worked, finally. He

9

agreed that any additional attention should be avoided. Her father was a very capable and successful businessman and was used to being in control of every situation, at work. Things were quite different at home. She loved and respected him very much but she made her own decisions. She would listen to him and would follow his advice if it seemed reasonable but would not blindly obey him, much to his chagrin. Her mother handled him differently, but equally effectively. She rarely argued with him but still made her own decisions. Her philosophy was that it was easier to let a man rant and rave and make all the declarations he wanted but in the end she would inform him of what she was doing and would discuss it no more. It worked great for them in that they were satisfied with their marriage and loved each other very much. But they didn't spend a lot of time together. They each had busy lives and seemed fine with only a few shared meals during the weak. Nora wanted more from a marriage. She wanted a true companion and for her husband to be her best friend. Even though they shared a different marriage than one she would want, her father was a good man. He would do anything for his family, and they were close. Under normal conditions, they had great discussions and he offered helpful insights. But his overprotective instincts overshadowed all other reason. Nora was independent and had been living on her own since finishing college. She even owned her own house. She wouldn't let a bad day send her back into the parental fold.

Nora called Monica, who had not heard anything yet because she had been running errands during the evening news. She and her husband, Stephan, said she could stay and would come to get her right away. That was a relief because her nerves could not take another ride with her mother, who refused to make left turns. By the time they actually got anywhere they were dizzy from circling and were inevitably late. Stephan and Monica wanted a full account of what happened. She told them the facts and tried not to visualize the act as she had been doing for the last few hours. She did not cry; her eyes were burning from all the crying she did earlier.

"I can't believe your dad let you leave after that," said Monica. "I'm surprised he didn't lock you in the house."

"I'm sure he considered it. But really, it wasn't that big of a deal. I just don't want to hide in my house while the local news is lurking outside," she said.

"And your dad didn't demand police protection?" Asked Stephan.

"No, I didn't really see that much. Plus he would consider his protection better," she said. Nora asked her family to not tell anyone, even other friends and family, where she was so there would be no interruptions. Her cell phone was silenced. There was only one call she was willing to take.

She and Monica talked about unrelated gossip and it felt good to speak words that didn't dredge up bad images. She would have to call Allen soon but put off talking about it again for just a little bit longer. Maybe after she told him it would stop replaying everything in her mind, but she could wait for him to call her when he was finished working for the day. Her mother called work for her because there was no way she could take care of patients in the high anxiety state she was in. Her nursing supervisor had been kind, after hearing a few details, and gave her personal time off work for the rest of the week. Nora wasn't sure she wanted to be gone that long, but could always call in a day or two and be scheduled for some shifts.

She was slowly working on a bourbon and coke when Allen called. Monica and Stephan busied themselves at the other end of the house while she quietly told him every detail of the day's events. He patiently listened and asked a few questions when she finished. Then he announced he was coming right home. She told him absolutely not, always the martyr. Nora convinced him she was fine and he should finish his business before coming home. In the end they compromised. He would finish everything he could tomorrow, and then would catch a flight tomorrow night and get in late. She still protested since she knew he had planned on staying several more days. Her arguments fell on deaf and very stubborn ears. Before they hung up he told her how much he missed her, and she him. As she brushed her teeth and changed into bedclothes, she reminded herself how lucky she was to have Allen. He seemed to be everything she wanted, and yet so different than all her previous boyfriends. It made her wonder if she had just always settled for something less, or if it just took maturity to realize what was important to her. She thought maybe seeing how wrong some of her other relationships were made this one feel all the more right. But he was almost too ideal. Everyone had weaknesses, but she had yet to see any significant ones in Allen. She really was waiting for the bomb to go off. They had only been together for a few months so it could still blow up. He seemed to be perfect for her. He was patient and caring. Though one negative aspect was his job, which required a good deal of traveling. His work wasn't terribly exciting. He was a products analyst for a pet food company. And he was gone more than he was in town. The time they spent together was good, though limited, since she worked a lot too. She tried to schedule her workdays when he was gone. She also used his away time to see her family and talk to friends so she wouldn't be making maintenance phone calls during their time together. As she lay down in the strange bed, she thought about them, together. They had discussed marriage in general but really hadn't been dating long enough to consider it. She really couldn't imagine what their lives would be like, with his traveling so much. It sounded a little too close to her parents' lives for comfort. They would have to do a lot of talking about expectations before taking their relationship to the next level. Nora lay there awake but enjoying the feeling of being in control of her own thoughts, as she was no longer tormented by the replays in her mind. Finally sleep took over.

She didn't know what time it was, but the house was dark and quiet. Nora was afraid but didn't know why. Something had woken her up. She tried to remember her dream, but it too was lost. She continued to lie there very still and controlled her breathing so she would stay calm. She heard a soft scraping sound outside, but there was no window in this room. She considered all the possibilities of the origins of the sound, but as is often the case, sounds in the dark can seem to be more exaggerated. Waiting an extra minute or so to make sure no shadows moved in the room, she quickly but quietly got out of bed. Nora didn't bother putting on shoes or getting dressed. Since she knew her friend's house well, she did not have to turn on any lights and luckily did not stumble over any furniture. When she found the living room Nora discovered she was not the only one who heard the noise. Petunia, the cat, was sitting on the window ledge looking toward the driveway. For no rational reason it made her feel better to see the cat there. She was a solid black cat with fur that looked and felt like velvet. She peered at Nora with big, bright questioning eyes. Nora had no answers, so she walked to each window very slowly and quietly to peek outside and find the source of the noise. There wasn't anyone on the front porch that she could see. It was very dark outside, the only brightness from the porch light. Outside the other windows she had to look for a very long time before she could start to make out shapes and detect any movement that wasn't from the light wind. As she got approached the second out of three windows in the room she bent down to peek out of the lowest panes. She stared into the darkness waiting for the shapes to make since in her mind. In the long seconds it took, an alarm was growing in her mind. Then terror swept over her so quickly it took another second for realization. The shapes that she had been studying were that of a face looking right back at her. This time Nora's voice did not fail her. She screamed with all the strength and loudness that should have been there earlier that day. She scared the face and herself. Both of them ran. She didn't know which direction the face ran in because she was already running into her friends in the dark hall as they were running to find out why she was screaming. Monica was calling 911 before Nora could get the whole story out and Stephan was looking out the windows in the dark just as she had done a few minutes earlier. Her heart was racing and she broke into a cold sweat. It was more than twenty minutes before the police arrived. Since the face did not enter the house and no one was hurt they didn't get the quickest response. They were lucky to get the one they did considering how many violent crimes go on in Memphis any given night. Nora gave the police a recap of what happened earlier that day and they were, of course, familiar with the event. The fact that she had been the witness of such a violent act only made them question her sighting of the face. They asked if she had taken anything to help her sleep or if she had been having a nightmare. Then they asked if she had been drinking the night before. Nora admitted to drinking one bourbon and coke, with a touch of guilt that she had used alcohol as a crutch to calm down. But since she knew she had not been drunk or dreaming, she would not back down or show any doubts to the officers. She could not give a very good description of the face because it had happened too quickly. She did know it was a man, and he had African American features. Beyond that she couldn't say for certain. They asked in which direction the man ran, but she didn't know. They told her there was no connection between this and the shooting to which she was the only witness. Nora could see how they came to that conclusion because no one outside her immediate family knew she was there, but she didn't believe it. They didn't argue with the police and let them leave after the usual warnings and suggestions. She could tell from the look on Stephan's face that he didn't believe the police theory either. She apologized to her friends for getting them involved. Being very polite, they responded that it was no trouble at all. But of course it was. She didn't know where to go or what to do. Monica tried to trace exactly who knew where she was, but the list was so short and unquestionably loyal to her that it left them nowhere.

two

Aching and burning. Her feet were so painful that it was the only thing she could think about. She sat down on the couch and bent over to slip off her shoes without even noticing the noisy television booming out the latest sit com. Her two teenage daughters were arguing over the phone.

"Mama, Tiffany's been on that phone for more than an hour. I was 'sposed to call Kenny an she won't give me the phone," said Sheila. The bickering continued but she ignored it as she stretched out her legs on the couch. She was so tired that she didn't have the energy to break up the fight. But she did it anyway, never letting exhaustion cause her to be apathetic to her children's needs.

"Tiffany, hang up the phone and do your homework," she said.

"Give it to me," said Sheila.

"No, give me that phone and you do your homework too," she said.

"Mama, I have to call Kenny," said Sheila.

"Don't argue with me Sheila Ray. Tiffany, give me that phone. Now, if I have to say it again you'll be sorry. I'm tired- been working all day so don't make me have to get up and whip the both of you. Do your homework and don't turn that radio on. TV's so damn loud I can't hear myself think." The girls knew she meant what she said so they handed off the phone and turned down the TV set to a normal level. As they were pulling out their books Tiffany realized that while she had been staying on the phone to keep Sheila from using it she had forgotten to clean up the kitchen. It was her day to do the kitchen. She knew that Sheila had already done her two loads of laundry that were her chores. If Mama went in the kitchen and saw the dishes and trash on the counters she would tear her up. Tiffany quietly walked into the kitchen, peaking through to the living room as she went. She could see her mother lying on the couch. It looked like her eyes were closed. Please, God, let her sleep for a little bit. Just long enough to get the kitchen clean. Maybe if she had been studying when her mother came home she would have been able to get away with it. Talking on the phone would not be a good enough excuse to avoid a beating. Quietly, she began cleaning as fast as she could because her mother would not

15

stay asleep long. Hunger would wake her up shortly. After about twenty minutes she finally slowed down and began breathing easily. She was finished and had made it without getting caught. Just a she was walking out of the kitchen she heard her mother asking Sheila where she was. Quickly she spun around and ran to the refrigerator. She could hear Sheila telling her she didn't know. As she was grabbing the ground beef she yelled to her mother that she was in the kitchen starting dinner. Her mother walked quickly to the kitchen.

"I thought I told you to do your homework," she asked, exasperated.

"I'm almost finished, Mama, but I got hungry and you were so tired. I just came in to get dinner started then I was going to go finish it," Tiffany said.

She thought it was strange that Tiffany was being helpful. Her story didn't really make sense but she was too tired to argue. Her children were a little out of control because she was always so tired when she was home. Mary Ray was forty-seven years old and had been a single parent since before her youngest daughter, Sheila, was born. The pressure of having two small children with a third on the way had been too much for her husband, Albert.

When she was six months pregnant he began to drink heavily. He'd always had a few beers when he got home from work, but nothing stronger. After she got pregnant with their third child he started to drink vodka, and a lot of it. Then started to feel really bad in the mornings when he got up, so he called in to work. A few weeks later he lost his job. This didn't convince him to stop drinking. Actually it caused him to drink more. Mary was getting bigger every day, it seemed, and was having a more difficult time at her job. Her feet were swollen when she got home. He was afraid she wouldn't be able to keep working much longer. How would he support the family without her? The more he worried about it the more he drank to forget. She begged him to stop drinking. He could find another job and then they could be just like before. But he didn't want to be like before. That's why he started drinking in the first place. Mary worked all day and cried all night. She tried hard to hide what was going on from her two children. They didn't really miss their father too much because he hadn't talked to them or played with them before he started drinking the vodka. They did miss their mother, who had always played with them and shown great affection for her children. Now she just cleaned and fed them as fast as she could, with very little talk and even less laughter because she didn't want them to see her cry. She knew it would scare them to see her cry. Tiffany was eighteen months old but seemed to notice everything. Mary would think she was doing a good job of hiding her worries but Tiffany would toddle over to her and pat her on the leg and with a serious expression say "OK Mommy." Then she would really lose it. Her son was four and was already a little man. He was always trying to get his father's attention but unfortunately it was usually the wrong kind. He would be showing off and spill something. All Albert noticed was Dedrick making a mess. So he would yell at the boy, then send him away. He never beat the kids but he couldn't have hurt them more if he had. Dedrick never stopped trying, but hid his disappointment from his mother. Albert got worse. He had a hard time getting to the liquor store for his vodka. Mary took the car to work so she didn't have to take the kids on the bus. They were staying at a women's house for fifty dollars a week. It didn't make sense to pay for childcare when they were so poor and Albert was home every day. At first he said he needed to be able to leave to find a job when he felt better. Then he was so drunk that she was afraid to leave her children with him. What if they needed something and they couldn't wake him up. No, that was fifty dollars they wouldn't be able to save. Mary finally refused to give him the money for the vodka or pick it up.

Albert was so mad when she walked through that door without his bottle he began to yell at her.

"Woman, are you stupid? You know I needs that bottle. I sees that belly all swolled out an' I knows you tired, but you gonna haf to go back out an gets me my bottle," Albert said. She hadn't forgotten that bottle. She had decided that if he was going to drink himself to death then she wasn't going to pay for it.

"Albert, I ain't going anywhere. Let me make you some coffee. Then I'll make you a nice dinner. I don't know when you ate last," Mary said. He got madder with every word.

"I don't care 'bout no food. If'n I don't gets that bottle I'll be dead afore midnight. Baby, I knows you don' wanna kill me; leave these kids with no daddy. I'll go get a job tomorrow but I won't live through the night if'n I don't got no bottle. Come on baby, please," Albert said. This was probably the nicest he'd been in a while. But he could see the resolve in her eyes. She wanted to believe him, felt sorry for him. She just couldn't make herself spend money on the juice that was killing him when she barely had enough money to feed her kids. She walked into the kitchen saying she was fixing supper. Albert's eyes glazed over as he stared at the coffee table. He didn't say another word. He wouldn't yell or beg anymore. Mary had just lost her last appeal to him. He had no feelings for her anymore at all. She made supper and fed the kids. She put a plate in front of Albert, but he didn't even blink. After she cleaned up the kitchen she fell into bed, absolutely exhausted. Albert could pout if he wanted to, but she knew she had done the right thing.

Albert waited until he could hear her snoring like a buffalo. Nothing was as loud as a pregnant woman snoring. He had already started shaking. It had been almost five hours since his last drink. He always finished the bottle about an hour before she got home. She always brought a bottle with her. Well, he knew now that she didn't care about him any more. All she cared about was those brats. That boy couldn't be his. He was too goofy. No child from him would be that clumsy. He tried to stand up slowly. The smell hit him and his stomach turned over. He must have wet himself earlier. He fought hard not to vomit. He was feeling really bad. Too much time. He needed that bottle now. He held on to the arm of the chair as he tried to straighten up. It took several minutes but he finally stood up straight. His head began to swim and nausea gripped him so quickly that he vomited before he could even take in a breath. He was on his knees, his whole body convulsing as he threw up the bile. There was no food. It was so violent he felt like is eyes would pop out. Then, after the last one he felt hot, thick liquid in his pants and running down his leg. That woman made him shit on himself. He had to get that bottle or it would only get worse. He would do this until he was dead. He stood up again after much effort. This time he didn't make the mistake of straightening all the way up. His knees were sore from hitting the floor so hard. He was surprised Mary hadn't heard him and come in to humiliate him. It was her fault, after all. Look at him. What kind of man was he now? She stole his manhood. He fumbled around and made his way to the bedroom he used to share with Mary. She was so big now they couldn't have both fit in the double bed if he'd wanted to. She was still snoring so she wouldn't hear him. He finally found her purse, but he didn't look in it yet. He was shaking so badly that he could barely hold it, much less find anything. He made his way to the bathroom. The light was on in there in case the kids needed to go in the night. He started to rummage through it but there were tissues and papers. He finally just dumped it out in the sink. Her wallet only had some change in it. He put it in his pocket. He found the keys to the house and car. Those went in the pocket too. Where was her money? He knew she got paid yesterday because she went to the store. Always buying food for those brats but wouldn't help him. He looked at himself in the mirror. His eyes were blood red. He face was ashen and his cheeks were sunken in. He looked like he was going to die tonight. He used to be strong and handsome but she stole his manhood and now he looked like an old man. An old, weak man. She must have her money in her bra. Every woman he knew hid their money in their bra. He was desperate now. His stomach was rolling again. It would only be a matter of time before it started again. He would have to buy two bottles because he might have to puke a few times before he got right again. He made his way back into the bedroom, holding on to the walls. She was still snoring, sleeping on her side. He just hoped it wasn't in the breast that was smashed against the bed. He slowly pulled back the covers because he knew he was too weak and shaky to get the money from her if she woke up. Her nightgown had a v-neck so it wouldn't be too hard. He lifted the neck of her gown a bit so he could look down it. She was wearing a bra to support her huge breasts. They were big before she was pregnant. Then after she breast-fed each child they dropped more. Now they were huge since she was so far along in pregnancy. The bra was tight. It would be difficult to get his hand in there. He thrust his hand in there with more force than he had intended. Luckily the money was right there. He pulled it out before she woke up. Her snoring had stopped. She was moving a bit. He stood as still as he could, barely even breathing. She wriggled her nose at the smell of him but exhaustion won over and she settled back in. Slowly he made his way back to the front of the house, fighting nausea and the urge to just lie down and rest for a while. But he knew it would only get worse. Then he might not be able to leave and he had to be gone before she woke up or she would take back the money and he would never get another bottle. She took everything away from him. His manhood, happiness, freedom. He didn't stop until he reached the car. The fresh air helped to bolster his strength a bit. After several minutes of searching he found the right key and unlocked the door. What would have taken him mere seconds before now took a supreme effort and several minutes. He started the car and backed out without ever turning his head. It made him sick to turn his head. He drove very slowly down the street because was still feeling sick and the motion wasn't helping. He drove up to the liquor store and got out, still clutching the small wad of money, still warm from his wife's breast. The lights were out and the doors were locked. How late was it? It must have taken him much longer than he thought to get out of the house. His wife shouldn't have been hiding her money from him. She never used to do that. She used to be a good wife and would bring her money straight to him on each payday. When had she stopped that? He hadn't noticed since she was bringing his bottles home to him. He rattled the door to see if it would open. No such luck. He looked around for something to throw through the window. He found half of a brick and was about to toss it when he noticed all the bars behind the glass. Even if he broke the glass he still would not be able to get a bottle out. Only stores in the poor neighborhoods had bars on the windows. He got in the car and started driving toward a richer area. He was driving so slowly that other cars were whipping around him. He didn't understand why everyone was driving so fast. Aren't they afraid of the police? Most people like him were. Anyone who had ever been harassed by the police because of the color of their skin knew the feeling of powerlessness. No one would take their word over that of a police officer, so they were at the mercy of that person in power. Some were honest and some were criminals but one never knew which was facing him. Power corrupts and racism compounds it. He pulled into the parking lot. It was a new building and the whole front of it was glass. It was closed but it was still well lit. There wasn't a single piece of trash in the parking lot. It was a good thing he brought his brick with him because he sure wouldn't find one here. He peeked through the window and spotted the vodka. He might just try one of those fancy kinds to see what all the fuss was about. He looked at the brick in his shaking hand and hurled it through the window. There was a loud crash and at the same time a shrill alarm sounded. He dashed in as quickly as he could on shaking legs and grabbed three liter bottles of Grey Goose, then stumbled back to the car. As he started the engine he thought he was doing great. He figured it took Memphis Police a long time to get anywhere other than lunch. He pulled out and started driving a bit faster this time. He was high on adrenaline. Albert Ray had taken back his manhood. He was free of the chains Mary had placed on him. He had a car, all the time in the world, money, and three bottles of fine vodka. He started to think of where to go to start drinking and get him right again when he heard the sirens. The police answered an empty store alarm in a rich area faster than they came for a shooting in progress in a poor area. So much for equality. What a joke. He drove a bit faster but so far the only blue lights he saw were ahead of him, on their way to the store. He was concentrating really hard so that he would blend in with traffic, but they were all driving so fast. Didn't they see those blue lights? He put a bit more pressure on the gas so he wouldn't get left behind. He wanted to get off this street where they drove so fast, so he turned off on a quiet residential drive and slowed down to a more comfortable pace. It must have been late. No one was out and all the houses were dark. Albert wound his way through the back streets toward the river. He would park his car on the bluff and taste his vodka. As he pulled into the poorly lit parking lot he noticed another car parked further down. There were probably a couple of kids screwing in the car. "Be careful, man," he thought, "or she'll trap you like Mary trapped me." He turned off the car and the lights. He quickly grabbed one of the bottles and fumbled with the top. When he finally got it open his mouth was like paste in anticipation. He turned it up and washed down all the tastes of foul mouth and vomit. He sat back and took a deep breath; waiting for the relief he knew would come. Warmness started spreading through his body that made him feel alive again. After several pulls and a few minutes the shaking stopped. He wouldn't die tonight. No, tonight he was living again. He had his manhood back and was free again. This vodka was smoother than what he was used to so he decided that he would drink Grey Goose from here on out. It didn't matter that it was expensive. He could just steal it. If he picked up an extra bottle next time then he would only have to break the glass twice a week. He was getting pretty warm now so he rolled down his window half way to let in the cool night air. The moon was at three quarters and there weren't any clouds so there was plenty of light on the river. The current was visible even from the car, highlighted by the silver light. He was really relaxing now, had his head back against the seat making plans for his life since he took it back. His eyes were closed so he didn't see the arm reach through the open window or the knife as it cut his throat. His eyes popped open at the same time as his hands grabbed at his neck. He couldn't breath. He began to feel cold again as his blood emptied out on to the seat. The man who cut him had been waiting for over three hours for some kids to come parking here. Instead he got some wino that smelled like hell. He reached over Albert and retrieved the two unopened bottles of Grey Goose. After gagging from the smell he went through Albert's pockets until he found the money. He figured Albert had to have some money if he had three liter bottles of fine vodka. Not much money and no sex with a teenage girl scared out of her pants, literally and figuratively, but better than nothing. He decided that he was probably doing this man's family a favor by getting rid of him. If he had any family. Christ, he smelled bad. He slipped the car out of park and into neutral and pushed it for a few feet until the ground began to sloop and the car picked up momentum. The splash wasn't as big as he would have thought. There was some gurgling and bubbling, and then it disappeared under the surface. With a current as strong as the Mississippi there was no telling where it would surface, if it ever did.

Mary felt the light starting to enter the room. She began to stretch and move because if she didn't get up now then she would be in bed all day. She couldn't afford to lose her job and besides, she really didn't want to see Albert acting pathetic all day. He would be really sick by now. She thought she had better get on up in case he needed help getting cleaned up before the children saw him. She wanted him to have some dignity. She went to the bathroom first and saw the contents of her purse in the sink and her purse on the floor. Her hand reflexively went to her breast where she always kept her money. It was gone. She began to panic and flew into the front room where she expected to find Albert passed out. All she found was vomit. She looked out the window and the car was gone. She knew it would be. All of her hopes and optimism were crushed. She went through the motions of cleaning up his mess and getting the children up and fed. She didn't know how she would make it through the day but she had no choice. Now more than ever she had to have her job. Mother's don't have the luxury of giving up.

She remembered those feeling just like it was happening all over again. She never knew what happened to Albert but she felt he was dead or he would have come back when the money was spent. He was lazy and would have taken the money from her again. She was serving the girls hamburger patties and instant mashed potatoes. The ketchup on the plate mixed with some of the grease and turned the potatoes pink on the edge.

"Have you girls seen Dedrick?" She asked as she took a bite of hamburger and onion.

"No, he ain't been home" Sheila answered. She didn't tell her mother that she had overheard a phone call last night in which he had plans to meet some people this afternoon. She didn't know what it was about because he was being very secretive. He didn't do drugs or drink. He wasn't in to that. Probably since Daddy had been a drunk. He remembered Daddy but didn't like to talk about it. Tiffany didn't remember him at all. Dedrick wasn't in any gang either. He managed to ride the fence by being friends with guys in several different gangs. He could probably do this because he played basketball. He played really well. Everyone likes someone who's talented. He was an easygoing guy, never fought. Lots of girls liked him but he didn't go for the super cute girls who collected boys like trophies. He liked smart, quiet girls. Because of this he wasn't competing for dates. He didn't do drugs because he was into his health. He had a part-time job at McDonald's so he could help his mother with the bills. She had a tough time when they were growing up but she never let them want for anything important, especially love. As soon as Dedrick could he started earning money to help the family. Sheila idolized her older brother. He was so tall, handsome, and smart. He was also very popular but didn't seem to notice. It never went to his head. Deep down he probably wasn't as self confident as he appeared to be. Now Tiffany, there was a girl who was every bit as confident as she appeared to be. She was mean and selfish, Sheila thought. They were just too close in age to get along. They even had some of the same friends. Still, she knew she would be lonely if it weren't for Tiffany, with her mother being at work all the time. They were finishing up dinner and clearing the table when there was a knock on the door. Mary answered the door. Two police officers were standing at the door.

"Can I help you?" She asked. She wasn't afraid of the police, had no reason to be, but she was wary. The police didn't knock on your door to give you good news. It crossed her mind that it might be something about Albert.

"Are you Dedrick Ray's mother?" The shorter officer asked. Her hand flew to her chest. Dedrick had never been in trouble before. Sheila and Tiffany were trying to peek around her.

"Yes sir, I'm Dedrick's mother. Is something wrong? Where is Dedrick?" She asked, her words tumbling out faster as she spoke.

"Ma'am, I'm so sorry to tell you this but your son was shot today in what appears to be a gang related conflict. He was taken to the hospital but didn't make it. We'll need you to come down to the Medical Examiner's office to identify the body," said the shorter officer. Mary went numb all over. The despair that had overwhelmed her when Albert left had returned. It couldn't be true. Not her baby. She heard a strange loud noise and instinctively turned around. She saw Sheila on the ground struggling to get her breath and a sound out of her wide-open mouth. When it finally came, a few seconds later, it was filled with such anguish that the tears were finally released and coursed down Mary's face. Tiffany was already sobbing. The officers felt awkward but tried to help Mary to the couch. Sobbing, she shrugged them off and kneeled on the floor by the girls and put her arms around them. She just kept saying to herself …it couldn't be true. Lord please, it can't be true.

three

It was now two-fifteen in the morning. There was no way Nora could go back to sleep. She had to think of some place to go where she would not put her friends in danger, or herself. She was feeling anxious to leave, and very vulnerable there. She couldn't just wait for this man to get a better plan and come back for her. Whoever it was wouldn't just give up because she screamed, and the police dropped by and left. This person must have gone to a great deal of trouble to find her and probably wouldn't take a chance of her moving tomorrow morning. She didn't want to leave town. It was out of the question for her to quit her job and take off. She refused to run scared from her life. She finally decided to check into a hotel for lack of better options, especially in the middle of the night, but didn't call Allen because there was nothing he could do to help at that hour. By the time he could get there, she would have figured something out. Nora made Monica and Stephan promise not to call him. They drove her to an ATM and she all but wiped out her account. She had seen enough movies to know credit cards were easily traceable, although the criminals she was trying to elude wouldn't be that resourceful. Still, she wasn't taking any chances. Nora had a friend who worked for one of the nicest hotels in Memphis, The Peabody. She and Courtney grew up together and were very close, so her husband wasn't at all mad when he answered the phone in the middle of the night. Nora called on her cell phone as they drove down Poplar Avenue to find an open fast food restaurant. Monica wanted something to eat. She liked to get a small order of French fries late at night. Nora knew cell phones could be traced, but was hoping whoever was following her wasn't that skilled. Courtney picked up the phone and said, "What's wrong?" She knew Nora well enough to know there wouldn't be a call in the middle of the night unless something was. Nora explained what had happened and that she needed a place to stay. Courtney immediately asked her to come and stay with them. Nora told her she couldn't put her family at risk as she thought of their eighteen-month-old daughter. Courtney tried to convince her they would protect her but she didn't understand the potential risk. She thought that what happened at Monica and

Stephan's house was a coincidence, but as she tried to convince Nora, her husband, Tom, told her it might not have been. Tom was a prosecuting attorney and recognized what Nora was saying was true and she could be in trouble. Nora talked to him on the phone and told him what her plan was. He suggested she leave town or call her father for help, but she refused. She didn't want her father telling her why he was right about her staying with him instead of Monica. After this all his worries would be justified and he would make it difficult for her to leave. Tom finally agreed staying in a hotel was her best choice for the night. Courtney said she should call Allen and have him come back to Memphis, but Tom understood her position of not wanting to put him in the middle of it, as she was sure he's felt about Courtney during particularly nasty trials. Courtney called the hotel and set everything up. The desk manager was surprised to get a call from one the hotel's accountants at just after three am. She told them Nora was her sister and couldn't stay with them because the baby had chicken pox and her sister hadn't been exposed yet. Nora was registered under Courtney's real sister's name. Courtney called her sister after calling the hotel so no mistakes would be made. Nora was sure they were being paranoid, but a good dose of paranoia wasn't a bad thing in this situation. She had her poor friends drive a circuitous route around Memphis to make sure no one followed them. At that time of morning there weren't many cars on the road. So when they were sure no one was with them, they headed downtown to the hotel. She didn't want any of the hotel employees to see her friends let her off, so she got out of the car half a block away and walked while they watched. She checked in at the front desk and prepaid for one night. Courtney, bless her, made sure the room was substantially discounted since it was for her sister. Nora had only one small overnight bag and was familiar with the hotel, so she didn't let a bellman take her up. Plus, the fewer people who saw her, the better. Someone could recognize her. She all but staggered through the lobby. Nora was so tired she must have resembled a zombie. She found her room without much difficulty and quickly bolted the door behind her. Instead of falling straight into bed, she ran a hot bath and soaked for twenty or so minutes. There had never been a stressful situation in her life that would prevent her from being relaxed in a hot bath. She wrapped a towel around her very warm body and unbolted the door just long enough to put out the do not disturb sign.

Then she fell into bed naked and exhausted. She didn't remember falling asleep or dreaming.

four

Something wasn't right. It just didn't make sense, Larry Whitman thought for the hundredth time tonight. He got home at eight-thirty that night and had been so preoccupied that his wife was worried about him. Something was bothering him about the Dedrick Ray case but he just couldn't seem to grasp which details his mind was rejecting. He made it through dinner with some small conversation for his wife and children. Martha appreciated the effort he made. It was difficult to be a homicide detective's wife. Larry was a good husband and father, but sometimes the stress would get to him. He took his job very seriously, which was one of the many reasons she respected him so much. But that kind of dedication didn't come without a price. It really wasn't a terribly unusual case. Kids were killed everyday in Memphis under similar conditions. The only reason this case received so much attention was because it happened outside an upscale restaurant. Children were killed weekly in drive-by shootings, daycare vans and as victims of domestic violence. They were mentioned somewhere in the first three pages of The Commercial Appeal newspaper but rarely made televised news. The Dedrick Ray case just didn't have the same feel as the others. It was still early in the investigation but what they found out about Ray so far didn't match the usual profile. He was African-American and from a poor area. He was also from a single parent home. That was where the similarities ended. He wasn't involved in gangs and had no history of any legal trouble. He was popular and well liked in school by teachers and students. He was an athlete who was dedicated to the team and his body. No one who knew him had ever seen him have anything to do with drugs and the coroner had called with some preliminary results, which included a clean drug screen. What had been the reason for the fight? Who was he fighting with? The witness stated the killer and accomplices appeared to be "gang-like", but would they really have known. The only witness to the murder was Nora Anderson, a twenty-six year old woman from an upper middle class background, and she didn't see much. Her only experience with gangs would be from fiction or news TV. Also, she was fairly traumatized by the event. Being a nurse she had probably seen her fair share of gore, but not violence. Lord help him if he ever got used to seeing a kid with his face blown off. Ray was dead before the ambulance got there, was probably gone before his head hit the ground. The nurse was upset about not trying to save him but the EMT's said it wouldn't have done any good. Too much damage. He continued to replay small conversations over in his mind. Just a snip here and a piece there, hoping to hit on the thing that was bothering him. He was just too damn tired. He took off his clothes and got into bed beside Martha but he didn't think he would be able to fall asleep. Sometimes it didn't matter how tired the body was, the mind still wouldn't let go. He had to lie there and try, was too tired to do anything else. Martha turned over and sat up in bed. She started rubbing his neck and shoulders to smooth away the tension. Slowly her strong hands and soft voice made bits and pieces of the day fall away. She didn't talk about anything in particular, just chatted and said things that made him smile or laugh, like funny things the kids had done or said that day. He felt warm and happy and tired. But mostly he felt loved. He fell deeply into sleep thinking he was the luckiest man alive. When she heard his breathing turn deep and rhythmic Martha gently lay down and smiled to herself. He was a wonderful, deeply caring man. It made her feel good that she could ease his frustration so easily. Martha fell asleep thinking that she was a very lucky women.

That feeling was tested when the phone rang at three-thirty am. Larry answered it on the first ring. Twelve years in homicide had brought quick reflexes and made him easy to wake.

"Whitman," he said, thickly.

"Sir, ah, I thought you might want to know about something that happened," said the young officer.

"It's a little late to make me play twenty questions. What is it?" Larry asked sarcastically, but not letting it sound annoyed. Many detectives had made the mistake of yelling at a less experienced cop in the middle of the night and had paid the price by not getting called again. A few needless calls were worth the many critical ones. Whitman had a reputation for being fair and honest. These were not traits that everyone considered positive.

"Sir, earlier we received a call about a peeper. When we got there he was gone. The residents couldn't see him well enough to give a description. I know this doesn't really have anything to do with you but since the woman who spotted the peeper is one of your witnesses..." the officer reported.

"Who?" Larry asked.

"Nora Anderson, from the Ray case. I just thought you might want to know. We thought it was just a coincidence but I guess you never know. It wasn't even her house. It was some friends she was staying with." The officer was rambling somewhat because he was worried he had made the wrong call. What if someone was trying to take out the only witness? He was basically waiting for Whitman to chew his ass when all he did was ask for the address and phone number. The officer quickly rattled off the numbers since he had just done the report, feeling slightly more confident about his decision since it didn't seem to be getting him into any trouble. Whitman heard the change in the timber of his voice and decided to let the kid have a break this time. He could have not called and then Larry would probably never have known. He thanked the officer and quickly got off the phone before the kid asked him if he made the right call. Larry would not go so far as to lie to him. Plus, who really knew if it was significant or just coincidence. Larry didn't believe too strongly in coincidence. It would all be related somehow. He got out of bed and went to the kitchen so that Martha could go back to sleep. He knew if he didn't go back to bed in the next thirty minutes she would get up and make coffee. He just wanted to call and talk to Nora for a few minutes to make sure she was okay and to encourage her to stay somewhere else tomorrow, just in case. He let the phone ring until voice mail picked up. He left a message for her to call and left his cell phone number. He hung up the phone but knew he wouldn't be able to rest until he checked it out. He went back to his room and as he began to get dressed he told Martha not to get up because he had to leave, but it should only be for forty-five minutes. She said okay but he knew she would be up before he got out of the driveway. She was the last of a dying breed.

He found the house quickly but it was empty. He wasn't the only one who had been here. The back door had been jimmied open. He called for back up before slowly moving into the house with his gun drawn. He did not expect to find anyone still there but didn't make any assumptions. The house was dark and quiet. He had just finished sweeping the house when his back up arrived. He'd found nothing except a surly black cat that nearly gave him a heart attack as she

30

jumped out of a closet when he opened the door. He left the officers to do the paperwork on the B&E while he went to the next-door neighbor's house. These days you couldn't count on a neighbor knowing your name much less emergency family contacts but he would try. Thankfully the residents were a friendly young couple that had been kind and helpful to many elderly neighbors in the area. He left with their parents' names and phone numbers. It took some time to calm down Monica's father but he agreed to come over and secure the house, and take that grouchy cat home with him. After Whitman assured him that they had not been in the house when it was breeched, Monica's father admitted to knowing where they may have gone. The neighbors had seen the three of them leave shortly after the police left the first time. No one had seen anything after that. Her father told him about a lake house a few hours drive from there. That was actually a great for place for her to go. He decided to get the local law to check on them in the morning since they wouldn't have had time to get there yet anyway, especially if they had stopped to get supplies. This time of year they probably wouldn't keep much there. When he walked through the door at home he was feeling better. She would be safe out of the city. His senses were assaulted by the delicious smell of muffins that had just come out of the oven. Life was good.

five

When Nora woke up, she had no idea where she was. All she could see was bright sunlight. She had forgotten to close the drapes before going to bed. Even with the sun streaming into the room as it was, she had still slept until eleven. Her muscles were sore from lack of movement during such a sound sleep. Her mind was clear and not at all groggy. She looked out the window at the old buildings of downtown. Memphis was an inviting city perched on the bluff of the mighty Mississippi River. When she sat on the bank and watched the river roll down to New Orleans it seemed so peaceful that it could almost be the 1800's again. Only now, instead of riverboats, there were barges transporting tons of raw materials way down south. Memphis was a beautiful city. Trees covered the entire area, with historic buildings boasting splendid architectural style. Old neighborhoods exemplified southern grace and charm. And Beale Street oozed the blues culture like nowhere else. Behind her cultured facade were some tarnish and cracks. She had not been well cared for or managed. Where cities like Atlanta moved forward with progress, Memphis seemed to slumber. She still had a tragically high crime rate and seemed to have a war going on in her streets. There were many sides to the conflict. To say that Memphis had racial injustices would be like saying that Martin Luther King Jr. was just a preacher. Unemployment and poverty ran high. Quality public education and opportunities ran low. Citizens elected officials who were corrupt and violated the rights of the very people who elected them. Corruption was nothing new for the Bluff City. It had a long and sordid history of manipulating the voters to elect the candidate willing to wield the most power, usually through bribery or terror. As new businesses moved into town so did people who expected some progress toward a more enlightened society. Theater and music bloomed, as well as the development of parks and downtown, which for years had seemed to decay. Scattered here and there were the newer buildings amongst the historic, many restored and loved. Traffic and people shared the streets as they went their way. Thousands of people would be at their jobs just as they were every day. Nora felt her world was the only one torn apart. She couldn't work.

She couldn't even go to her own home. She was feeling very sorry for herself when she noticed the ringer on her cell phone was turned off. There were several missed calls, including some from her mother. Nora called her back first. Her mother was frantic when she answered the phone.

"Where are you? I've been calling all morning and no one has answered the phone," she said.

"I called your cell phone and Monica's house."

Nora told her what happened and where she was, but was very concerned her friends didn't answer their phone since her mother started calling them at seven am. They didn't normally leave for work until closer to eight. Laura Anderson wanted to come and take her to the airport.

"We could go on a trip together. We'll find a nice hotel with a private beach and stay for a week or two until this is over," she said.

"I'm not leaving town. This is ridiculous. I'm sure everything will blow over in a day or two," Nora said. She could hear Sam in the background asking where she was. When her mother told him, he took the phone from her.

"If you won't stay here then let me send some corporate security guys to your house. They will keep you safe," he said.

"Dad, you should have some guys stay at your place but I don't want to be under house arrest," Nora said. After last night she was more convinced than ever she should stay away from them. She wanted some privacy, and didn't want to be responsible for anyone else's safety in case she was wrong. Because while she knew seeing a violent murder was a big deal, Nora couldn't reconcile what was happening now. Gangs wouldn't have the resources to track her to the Ross' house. Staying in a hotel, under an assumed name should have been overkill. But somehow it didn't feel that way. Calling in Sam's big guns was an option but it came with strings. She would definitely go that route if she were convinced there was more than paranoia going on. Until then it wasn't worth putting herself under her parent's thumbs.

Nora showered and dressed. Her stomach was growling, but she wasn't sure it was safe to leave the room. She finally decided to order room service. She ordered a turkey club sandwich, a cup of shrimp gumbo, and a club soda with lime. She didn't know the server and saw no sign that he knew her. She paid him in cash and gave a twenty percent tip, or as close as she could get to it with limited change. She didn't want to be discussed by the employees as either cheap or generous. She ate only half of the sandwich and the entire gumbo. After carefully wrapping the other half of the sandwich, she put it in the ice bucket, making her own cooler. An hour of boredom later she convinced herself she was being very paranoid and went down to the lobby to get a newspaper and maybe watch the ducks swim around.

The Peabody was famous for its ducks that swam in the lobby fountain. She settled herself on a settee and was glad she had put on make-up and paid a little attention to her hair. It was shoulder length and dark blond but had just enough curl to make it look unruly if not frequently tamed. She was taller than average for a woman at 5'8". She had a slim but athletic build for which she could thank her father's genes. She didn't get the voluptuous build that her mother gave her sister. There were many business men and women in suits going through the lobby on their way to one of three tasty lunch spots in the hotel. And while Nora tried to blend in, her attractive Nordic features made her notable. She felt conspicuous in jeans and a cream blouse. She ordered an iced tea so maybe she would feel a bit more natural. There were a few tourists milling about. She pretended she looked like them, started reading the paper, and forgot about all the professionals passing through. The story she was interested in was on the front page. At least there wasn't a picture of her. Her mother had saved her from that. However, Nora's name was mentioned in the article. The police hadn't tried very hard to prevent it. They assumed that it was just another case of gang bangers and that they wouldn't care about a witness, or wouldn't be resourceful enough to track her down. Nora disagreed. She wasn't sure why, but she didn't think this was another gang dispute. It was an odd place for a gang fight. Mostly Overton Square, where the restaurant was located, was known for having the occasional transient pester for money. People didn't walk around alone and were careful about where they parked their cars, but it was not so rough that one feared for his life, especially at lunchtime. Also, where was the security guard? There was usually one around the restaurant because the clientele tended to be more upscale. If many of their regular patrons were robbed on their way in or out they would lose the business that has kept them open, in spite of the fluctuations of criminal

34

activity in that neighborhood. Another thing that bothered her about the whole situation was that it wasn't a drive-by, or a spontaneous eruption of violence. It was a brief verbal fight and a cold-blooded murder with a get-away car. Her last reason for questioning the obvious conclusion was one that she wouldn't share because it wouldn't make sense to anyone else. It was the look in those eyes. It wasn't raw anger and hatred. There was an intelligent malevolence. Whatever the motivation, she had to figure out a plan because she couldn't stay in a hotel for the rest of her life. Nora had already made up her mind not to leave town and she couldn't very well stay hidden effectively in her own city for long. Eventually someone would recognize her or she would lose her job. She was beginning to feel acute anxiety again so she stopped thinking about her job or even about tomorrow. She had to decide what to do right now and would trust the other things in her life would fall into place. She went back up to her room and called the police. One of the detectives, Larry Whitman, had given her his card. He wasn't in when Nora called but she spoke to another detective named Thompson. He was very dismissing on the phone and actually told her that she was to only call him if she remembered anything else about the crime or had any information that would help solve the crime. His attitude converted her anxiety to anger in a snap.

"Do you realize, Mr. Thompson that because of your inability to control the press I cannot go home and am forced into hiding?" She said.

"Has something happened at your house that I don't know about?" He asked.

"No, but only because I haven't gone home to make myself a victim," she said.

"You're making this out to be much more than it really is. Gangs shoot at each other all the time. The only reason the press made such a big deal about this one was because of the location," he said.

"Someone tried to break in to my friends' home where I was staying last night. That should tell you something," she said.

"I know what happened last night. All that tells me is you had a very unlucky day yesterday," he said. Well, at least he didn't suggest she had been dreaming or drinking. The only way he would believe she was in danger was if something happened to her. Nora refused to be bait. She didn't trust the police to arrive in time to save her. She also didn't trust herself to be able to react if the need arose. What if she panicked again and was frozen solid while criminals got into her house and killed her. No way. She finished up the conversation by telling Detective Thompson she would continue to hide until they did their job, which was to catch the criminal. He asked her where she was staying so he could tell Whitman when he got back. She refused to tell him on principle. If he was so sure it was over then he didn't need to concern himself with her location. When he said goodbye he made no effort to hide his annoyance with her. It only reflected the way she felt. Nora looked out the window and thought about Allen. She felt isolated and really wanted the company. His plane wouldn't arrive until after eleven tonight. She wanted him to stay with her when he got back in town, but there was no way to get in touch with him right now as he was on a plane. He would assume she was still at Monica's house, but would call after he landed and she could update him then. She tried to call Monica and Stephan's house again and only got their voice mail. She didn't leave a message. No answer from their cell phones either. Nora was worried about them. But they knew what they were dealing with and did not for a minute think the attempted break-in was a coincidence. They were smart and would hopefully take precautions. Monica and Stephan knew her very well, and she was not one to make a big deal about something without a very good reason. She assumed they were staying with either family or friends. They had many of both in town.

She had to take some kind of action or go mad. Her biggest problem with doing something was she didn't have a car available. Memphis had very poor public transportation. Basically everyone drives who possibly can. She called her sister, Helen, who had her car. Nora thought about getting her to switch cars, but what if something happened to Helen because she was driving her car. Nora couldn't take that chance. She asked Helen to pick her up a few blocks from the hotel. They drove around for a while, looking for quiet streets so they could tell if anyone followed them. They finally felt confident they weren't being followed but decided not to go to Helen's house anyway. Even though her name and number were private, they didn't want to take a chance. She called a friend and had Nora drop her off there. Her friend would drive Helen home in a couple of hours. Helen didn't seem to mind but Nora was getting tired of having to ask for so many favors.

Everything was so complicated and taking did not come naturally to her. In life, there were takers and givers. And Nora was undoubtedly a giver. Or, at least, she had been.

Nora went and filled her car with gas because she didn't know when she might have to bail out of this mess. She drove back to the hotel because frankly she didn't know what else to do. Just getting the car had been so stressful she didn't feel enthusiastic about venturing anywhere else. She parked herself and went straight to her room. She had a few messages waiting on the voice mail. Courtney had called to see if everything was okay. She wasn't at work today because of the baby's chicken pox. Monica had called to let me know they had gone to the family lake house at Pickwick, which was about two hours away. Courtney had given them the number and Nora was glad to know they were okay. Everything had been going so smoothly that she began to think this was blowing over and maybe she had been a little paranoid. She went down to the lobby gift shop to find a novel to help pass the time. Allen still wouldn't be there for hours. Nora no longer felt out of place in the lobby. Most of the suited beings were gone. It was close to five so the lobby was filling with tourists to see the ducks go up to their penthouse via the elevator. Nora was having a good time poking around the gift shop, playing with anything playable and laughing at the ridiculous prices. She took her time picking out a book, which turned into three novels, two romances, and one mystery. If she were going to be off work she may as well enjoy it. She paid with cash, of course, and wandered out to watch the ducks. The lobby was very full so she went up one flight of stairs to the mezzanine level and watched from the balcony. Nora had always enjoyed people watching and was doing more of that than watching ducks, which she had seen dozens of times. Her eyes scanned the crowd and she couldn't help but smile. Just being at The Peabody made her smile. She had been going there for events and occasions since it reopened in 1981. She felt very comfortable there. Many of the tourists hadn't been before and stared wide-eyed at the beauty and luxury it emanated. The people moved very stiffly as if they were in a china shop. They looked around so much it was a wonder they didn't trip over something. Once the ducks were gone most of the people headed over to seats so that they could ogle the hotel without feeling so conspicuous. It was then, with the crowd dispersing, that she saw a cluster of three men scanning the crowd with purpose. One looked straight at Nora and pointed to show his friends. Her gut instinct was to run, but she tried to rationalize she feelings. As soon as they realized she was returning their stare, they started to move quickly, glancing back every few steps. Nora started to run for the elevators that would take her up to the safety of her room. She didn't even think about the possibility that they could have jumped on the elevator on at the lobby level and would be waiting for her as she got on. She did, however, begin to worry about being followed to her room. It was the only safe place she had. Nora had to assume it was still unknown to her enemies or surely they would have just waited for her there. She jumped on the first elevator that opened. It was going up. She rode to the floor on which a woman and three fighting kids stopped. Nora got on and road back down to the lobby level. She would have to take her chances at being noticed. Surely no one would hurt her with all those people around. Also, she wanted her pursuers to see her back downstairs because then they would hopefully assume she was not staying there or she would have gone up to hide in her room. At this point, Nora was willing to take a risk at being caught rather give up her secure place. She would rather face this now, expecting it, than to be woken from a sleep. She watched people carefully and strolled around the lobby, not straying too far from the crowd. Normally she hated crowds but today she hoped they would be her salvation. She periodically looked up to the mezzanine level. She saw a man scanning the lobby. The look on his face was not one of the casual observer, but one of a predator. He was not the man she saw murder another. He couldn't even be part of the gang. The face she was reading, as well as the other two that were searching for her, was light skinned, they were not youths and they were not dressed in the manner of one who hangs out in the streets. These were nicely dressed men in their early thirties. He saw her. Nora's heart jumped and breath came faster. She kept watching him as he started to motion toward her. She followed his gaze until she could see one of the other men begin to make his way around the lobby to get to her. Nora's wish to be noticed had been satisfied, but now she was pursued again. She ran down the hall and quickly turned into Café Espresso. It was crowded, as usual, but there wasn't a wait yet. Luckily there was no hostess standing at the front. She stopped running and walked quickly and confidently across the cafe, following a server to the back, in the kitchen. As soon as she was back there someone noticed her and told her that she must go back out into the cafe. Nora gave the server a terrified, pitiful look as she began to tell him she was a hotel guest and was being harassed and chased through the hotel. He looked a little doubtful but called the manager over. While he listened to her story the server she talked to first went back out to continue working the busy shift. He came back a minute later and asked her to describe the men. Nora described two of them as best she could. He interrupted her attempt to describe them completely. She had given enough evidently because he told the manager there were two men questioning the customers and other servers. They were describing Nora. The manager quickly called security. She begged him to take her out the back or to hide her in case they were as bold as she was. He reluctantly took her to the back door. He then asked for her room number or name so security could get a statement from Nora later. She told him she was sorry but she had lied. She told him she was not a guest of the hotel. He tried to grab her arm but she had already started to run. He took a few steps into the cold alley but stopped. It must have occurred to him that she had done nothing wrong except lie to get faster help. She hadn't stolen anything. When security arrived the two men walked quickly out the side door. Security didn't chase the men because they didn't really know what was going on. All they knew was two Caucasian men were bothering customers and chasing a woman. They didn't see a woman and since the men left they were no longer bothering customers. The security officers didn't get a very good look at them, but they had a vague description from the server and a few helpful customers. The officers on duty passed the word around and everyone, even bellman and the concierge would be especially cautious and report anything out of the ordinary. Nora had raced down the alley and then walked casually through a side door and straight to the elevators. As she reached her room she realized she still had her gift shop sack of books. The bag was all mangled. She laughed at the absurdity of her mission. She had risked her life to get novels to her room, and by damn, she had done it. It was then the phone rang. She answered. It was Courtney. Nora told her what happened. Courtney called the head bellman and got the gossip from the hotel's side and called her back. It made Nora feel a little better that everyone had been alerted. She called Helen to make sure she had made it home okay.

Nora lay down on the bed to read and wait for Allen to call. She read the same sentence four times before she put down her book and started thinking about what had just happened. Who were those men and what did they want with her? Did they want her or were they working for someone? Were they criminals or could they have been police? She hadn't seen any weapons. They hadn't shown any kind of identification while questioning the customers in the cafe. They didn't stick around to explain things to security. Based on those facts she decided they were not from any law enforcement agency, at least not one that had her best interests at heart. Those men had not been gang bangers. As a law-abiding citizen her first instinct was to call the police. She didn't call. She had no desire to get into another verbal debate with Detective Thompson. Also, no one knew she was staying there, but she had called his office. She thought she had blocked caller ID, but maybe that didn't work with the police. She was giving herself a headache playing 'what if'. She dug some aspirin out of her bag and drank a whole glass of water. Nora realized she was hungry so she ate the other half of her sandwich. At least she wouldn't have to worry about getting dinner tonight. It was seven-thirty. There was nothing on TV so she watched a news channel for about an hour. As soon as the inevitable arguments between experts started, she turned it off. She read until ten and turned on the local news. The murder was mentioned briefly. They did not yet have a suspect in custody, but had several promising leads. Right. She bet they did. Nora continued to watch TV until Allen called. He was still at the airport. He said he was coming to get her. She told him she had to stay. She didn't feel safe anyplace else. Nora knew he thought she was being ridiculous, but at least he didn't make the mistake of saying it.

"Could I just stay with you, then?" He asked.

"Please stay with me," she said. If he hadn't wanted to stay with her, she knew she would have cried. So much for being an independent woman. Nora felt so alienated. She couldn't wait for him to get there. He got a cab and came straight to the hotel. She felt a little bad that she hadn't gone to pick him up but couldn't get past her fear of leaving the room.

It seemed like forever, but Allen finally arrived. Nora had told him the room number. She asked him not to stop at the desk but to just go up and if anyone asked, his wife had already checked in and was waiting. She also gave him the name she was listed under in case he had any trouble.

Earlier, Courtney's husband, Tom, had offered to go by her house with Courtney's key to make sure everything was okay. She had just called as Allen knocked on the door.

"Courtney, hold on just a second, someone's at the door," she said.

"Don't you dare answer it!" Courtney said.

"I'm sure it's Allen but I'll check first," Nora said, as he knocked a second time. It was Allen. She threw herself into his arms and things felt normal for the first time in two days. She was so relieved she almost cried, but didn't want him to think she couldn't handle this problem. The truth was she didn't think she could. Nora was beginning to doubt her decisions and her perception. She needed some reassurance. Allen was the best person for that job. He cared about her and was a little more objective than she was. She went back to the phone and apologized to Courtney for the delay. Nora assured her it was Allen and that she was okay. Courtney told her Tom hadn't seen anything out of the ordinary and that everything was locked up tight. Nora asked her to thank Tom and then promised to call back tomorrow. After making sure Nora was okay, he went over to the mini bar and made them each a bourbon and coke. He sat down on the bed and waited for her to tell him everything. She didn't want to even think about it for another minute, so she started to explain things slowly without much detail. He let her get away with that for a while since he had heard about the first day over the phone. When she reached a part with which he wasn't familiar he began asking questions. Finally Nora told him everything, every detail, every impression of the events. He was upset that her life could have been in danger and she didn't call him.

"Damn it, Allen, I don't want to have to call you every time I get myself into something difficult to handle," she said.

"Nora, you can't always solve things on your own. Everyone needs help sometimes. Would you want me to go through what you have been without my calling you?" Said Allen.

"I know you're right. I just can't help but wish that I could handle it all without bothering you," she said.

"You aren't bothering me. I like to know that you need me every once in awhile," Allen said.

"Every once in awhile? Allen, it seems like need you all the time," she said. And she almost believed it. Nora needed and wanted help on some levels, but still didn't feel that dependent on Allen. She felt stupid about it but she didn't want to cross that chasm with him yet. She needed to maintain some independence from him. They hugged each other tightly, each reassuring the other. It was difficult to be apart so much, especially in the early stages of their relationship. When Allen was traveling they began to get intolerant of each other because it was easier to miss someone who was bugging you. They were both stubborn. He laughed at her for being so headstrong and independent. She glared at him. He had a way of making her feel foolish when she was frustrated with him. Nora didn't switch gears quickly so she liked to sulk for a while after being irate. Allen never let her do that. He always made her laugh at herself. It's hard to stay mad when a grown man is grinning at you like a twit. She would give in and smile in spite of herself. He leaned over, grabbed her arm, and pulled her out of the chair she was sitting in and onto the bed. They hugged each other tightly and she sighed with contentment. He stroked her hair and rubbed her neck. She tilted her head back and looked at him, longing for him to kiss her. Evidently he was familiar with that look because he did. The kiss was very sweet and gentle, at first. It had been a while since they'd been together and they felt the distance. The transition from embrace to more was tentative. Then it was as if their bodies took over and reached across the chasm created by over thinking. Their kisses deepened as their hands began to explore each other. His mouth delved deeply as if he were trying to devour her. She felt excited flutters in her stomach, running her hands down his arms and back and through his hair. They pressed their bodies as close as they could get to each other. Her mind filled with happiness as her body filled with passion. She let the cloud of fear and stress float away. Neither of them tried to accelerate things, just enjoying the pleasure of touching each other for the moment. Then the kisses and caresses became hungrier, both needing more. They worked their clothes off, slowly, almost like contortionists in slow motion. Their hands sought each other, every inch of her body and soul screaming with desire for him. She felt herself being equally covered by his desire. Soon after, they were both wound in each other's arms and legs under covers whispering words of amazement at how good it was being together. They fell asleep to each other's breathing and did not separate until the combined body heat made it too warm to be comfortable. Even while sleeping apart, they kept a hand or foot touching to reassure the other was still there.

six

The next morning went by quickly. Nora ordered room service for breakfast. She had no concern of being recognized because Allen ordered and received the food while she was dressing in the bathroom. She began to relax, no longer as afraid. Everything that had happened over the last few days seemed so far away. When Allen began talking about a plan, she found herself minimizing the danger. Nora wanted her life back. Allen's presence reminded her of the independence she had enjoyed. She had a good career, a great relationship, loyal friends, and a loving family. She was very content with her life and continued to strive to meet the goals she set for herself. Those things weren't given to her. She had worked hard to get where she was and to stay there. It took work to maintain friendships and family relationships.

Nora wasn't a spy and didn't have any covert training. The fact that she remained unfound and was never harmed told her that maybe no one was really after her. Maybe the men who chased her in the lobby were with someone's private security. Maybe she just looked suspicious because she was so paranoid. She could dream up scenarios all day, but none of them would give Nora her life back. She decided right then she was going to take it. Courtney had reported that Tom found nothing amiss at her house. Since it was a Thursday, Allen really needed to at least check-in at his office for a few hours, especially since he left Houston early. He refused to go at first, but she told him she didn't need the room anymore. And since they were leaving she could drop him off at work for two or three hours and then pick him up. Nora told him she needed to visit her parents. She really needed to reassure them that everything was fine and the best way to do that was for them to see her looking okay. It took a lot of fast-talking and rationalizing, but she was good at it so he agreed. Deep down everyone wants to believe nothing can happen to them or their loved ones. Convincing people they are overreacting is easy, especially if they haven't seen anything happen first hand. She checked out at the desk, paying for the second night in cash again. Allen went out to get the car. While she waited at the door it took so long that she was afraid maybe somehow, someone had vandalized her car, but it was fine when he drove up. It bolstered up her courage and validated her assurances that everything had blown over just like the police said it would. They knew more about these things anyway, right? She noticed Allen was wearing a gray suit as he got out to open her door. She loved a man dressed in a suit. It made him look so sexy. She watched him walk the whole way into his building. She really hated to see him go, even for just a few hours. But he never would have let her go home if he had stayed with her. That's exactly where she went. Nora needed to see for herself that everything was fine. She also wanted more than one change of clothes. She could get supplies, including uniforms, and take them to Allen's apartment. They had decided she should move in with him for a few days, then she could go back to work more quickly.

seven

Standing in her kitchen caused an odd combination of peace and anxiety. The peace coming from the sense of control she had in familiar surrounding, where she was in charge. Anxiety, which was rooted from the fear of that control being taken away. It wasn't too hard to imagine the sanctity of her home being crumbled. It had happened before, except in a much safer place. When she was eight years old her family's home felt like the safest place on Earth. That security was the basis of the confidence Nora felt as she sneaked back to the party her parents were having, even though she had been sent to bed. She felt she was old enough to be there, despite what her parents thought. Nora could hear talking and laughing from the other side of the house and the patio. She didn't want to be sent back to her room so she stayed in the darkness, following a path to the back yard. She planned to circle the backside of the patio so she could watch but not be seen. The path was dark and made of brick, lined on one side with lattice covered in vines and the other with azalea bushes, thick with blooms. It was a spring night, with unseasonably high temperatures. A warm breeze swirled her long, blond hair and nightgown. Every few minutes it blew just a little harder than the last. The air was thick with humidity. A storm was building, but that meant nothing to an eight year old on an adventure. The pathway opened up into a small brick walled garden. Just on the other side of the garden was another pathway that led to the patio and pool. She could cut through and get close enough to watch the party and not be seen through the bushes. As she crept closer to the garden she heard voices. She didn't know what they said, only that they were angry. She peeked through the bushes to see who was fighting. Nora didn't hear her father's angry voice so she thought it safe to look. The softly rumbling thunder and more insistent wind gusts began to get her attention, but curiosity won out. There were three men standing and one man sitting on a concrete bench. The man on the bench looked scared. Nora began to be afraid. She had never seen grown-ups fight. They were terrorizing the man, trying to get him to do something he didn't want to do. Then he started to cry and said "not my little girl". She'd heard enough and only wanted to get back into the house. She wasn't old enough to go to the party after all. She hoped she was never old enough to go to a party like that. Nora turned and started to run but tripped on uneven bricks before she had taken two steps. She screamed as she fell and cut her leg on the bricks. Before she realized it, the three men were standing over her. One man was trying to help her up, but she pulled away from him and looked at all of them with such terror there was no doubt she heard their conversation. One of the men grabbed her arm and pulled her up. She stood there, afraid to move, with blood dripping down her leg. Maybe if she had screamed for help someone would have heard her. The patio wasn't too far away, just right through the bushes and down a path. Maybe if she had pulled away and run she could have made it to the house or someone might have seen or heard her. Nora would never know because she was unable to do anything but stand there, barely breathing. She wanted to move but couldn't. It was as if her arms and legs were bound. Even the lightning didn't make her flinch. After a short discussion between the men, she was picked up and taken to the wall around the property and passed over from one man to the other, while the third man retrieved the car. Nora was thrust in the car as the rain started coming down. She never knew what happened to the man on the bench. She never saw him again. That was only the beginning of her terror. She shook her head violently to make the memory of that night stop. She couldn't relive that again right now. No need to take on the demons of the past when there were plenty in the present.

Nora walked into the den, put down her purse, and began turning on lights, glancing in the mirror as she passed. She looked tired, felt older. Fear and stress seemed to speed up aging. She looked around and could find nothing out of place, but something seemed wrong. She was out of sync with her life and routine, and realized it may never return. She decided long ago not to let fear control her life, but she couldn't completely insulate herself from its effects. Quickly putting together a light lunch she thought about what she should pack. She was tempted to just stay there but knew Allen would never let that happen. It was too much like she had traded her father for a boyfriend who was equally overprotective. She ate a few bites of her lunch quickly because she was shaky, but she was no longer hungry. She dumped the rest down the sink, flipped on the disposal, and washed it away. Tom was right. Nothing looked disturbed. Normally she would have opened the blinds but today wouldn't be here long enough to justify the effort. Actually she hadn't closed them before she left because she was only going to lunch. Helen must have closed them, or Tom could have, to keep nosey eyes out of her home. Nora grabbed a bag and started to throw stuff in it. She grabbed several hangers with uniforms on them. It made her so sad and angry to have to leave her home. She had made two trips out to load the car and was doing a final run-through of the house when the phone rang. She picked it up instead of letting it go to voice mail.

"Hello?" She said. "Hello... Hello?" Nothing, then click, they hung up. She went in the kitchen to wash out the lunch dishes and to gather the trash to take out. She quickly cleaned out the refrigerator, not leaving anything that might spoil in the next few days. Nora didn't want the next time she came home to be a confrontation with mold and chunky milk. She was concentrating on the task at hand when a noise stole her attention. The hairs on the back of her neck began to stand on end before her conscious thoughts even recognized the sound. There was someone trying the latch on the front door. It was the same sound she made all the time because the weather stripping on the door made it difficult to open all the way, even when it was already cracked. She knew she hadn't locked the door; she probably hadn't even closed it all the way since it was so hard to open and close. Nora dropped what she was doing and ducked down behind a counter. Luckily she had already turned off several lights and quickly reached up to turn off the kitchen light so it wouldn't attract anyone. She jumped as she heard the loud noise of someone forcing the big door open. She was hoping a neighbor would see strangers at her house and call the police, but it probably wouldn't happen. Most of her neighbors worked during the day, which is why they all had alarms. Of course it didn't do much good to have a security system if it wasn't armed. Hell, she hadn't locked the door, hadn't even closed it all the way. She crawled from the kitchen to the dining room, which was, thankfully, dark. She didn't use it very often so the door to the entry hall was closed. There was a closet in the entry hall, and if she could get there she could get out the front door. Nora would have to get far away before they noticed her because screaming outside would probably not get anyone's attention. All she kept thinking about was how Allen was going to kill her when he found out. She was so stupid. This wasn't the first dumb thing she'd done and she sure hoped it wouldn't be the last. She could hear the occasional whisper, which told her there were at least two of them. They headed to the living room first because the light was on in there. She was so glad the kitchen light was out because it was too close for comfort. The living room opened up into the entry hall so she couldn't try to sneak out yet. She was listening close to the door for whispers and footsteps. She was listening so closely that she almost screamed when the whispers were suddenly right on the other side of the door. Nora quietly moved as fast as she could under the dining room table. There was no place else to hide in that room. Thank goodness on her mother's last visit she had put on the "old lady" tablecloth. It was lacy and white, but it was also long. In this dark room no one would be able to see her unless they got down to floor level and looked under. She was counting on their laziness. The door pushed open quietly. She held her breath. She saw the feet of one man. Damn it. If they split up she would never know when it was safe to run out. It was only a matter of time and frustration before they got angry and began looking more carefully. She didn't have any idea of where to hide in her own house. Her security was built on the premise that no one got in the house, or that if they did she would have some notice to get her gun out of the safe in the bedroom closet, call 911, and hold off the bad guy until the police could get there. She had never even considered this scenario. Luckily the feet continued to walk slowly into the kitchen. She crawled to the edge of the table nearest the door to the entry hall. The man had left it halfway open. It made it easier to hear the voices and footsteps, but riskier to come out of hiding. Nora knew she had to chance it. She couldn't sit there waiting under the table until they pulled her out like a child who hides to get attention from the adults talking after a meal. She crawled to the door and peaked out. The hall was clear, but she couldn't hear any voices to let her know where they were. Her house wasn't that big so she knew they would be back up front very soon. She was getting off her knees as she started out the hall door when she saw the legs of another man. He had to be sitting on the edge of her porch in front of the door. She couldn't believe how blatant these people were. They didn't even pretend to be concerned with neighbors or a police patrol, not that she believed the police would follow through with the drive-bys they promised. Nora didn't blame them. There were too many criminals out there for them to catch. She quickly ducked back into the dining room. It would have to be the back door or nothing at all. Also, getting away in her car was out. She wouldn't have a chance of even reaching it much less driving off before the man on the porch could catch or shoot her. Now, she hadn't actually seen a single weapon yet, but she firmly believed they were present. These men appeared to be professionals and were not shy. She couldn't imagine their being so bold as to walk into someone's home without knocking or announcing themselves if they were anything but dishonest. Most, if not all, criminals have a weapon of some sort. These men looked as if guns would be their weapons of choice. She ducked and ran into the kitchen and peaked around the corner into the living room. No one was in there now. They must be in the back of the house going through her bedroom and office. She suddenly felt queasy at the thought of them going through her things. She pushed it aside in her mind. Thinking like that would get her caught, and probably killed. She ran through the living room and made it to the laundry room that led to the back door. If she could just get out without making any noise she would be free. This door didn't stick as badly as the front, but it sure wasn't silent. She didn't use it as often and had never really paid any attention to the noise level of opening and closing it. Carefully turning the deadbolt, it made a soft click. She turned the lock on the doorknob. It was silent. Her nerves were taught to the breaking point as she turned the knob very slowly. It clicked open and she pulled as hard as she could, but very slowly. It didn't budge. She leaned back and pulled again. It started to pull but she couldn't make herself give it a real tug because she was terrified of the noise. Finally time motivated her into action. She knew this was her only chance of escape and the window was closing fast. Nora jerked it open. It made some noise, though how much she couldn't say for sure since every sound was magnified to her. She stepped out quickly and pulled it closed. She ran through the back yard to the fence, which was six feet tall. She would have to climb it to get out of the yard since she couldn't go around front and the gate was locked with the key safely hanging in the laundry room. She used one of the cross pieces of wood on the fence to boost herself up some, and then she threw her leg to the top letting her ankle grab the edge. Then she pulled the dangling leg up to the top. She did it, but it sure was harder than she remembered it being. She had only climbed a fence once before in her life and it was to escape the police when she was seventeen. A keg party she was attending got busted. She literally flew over the fence that night. There were several of them that could have qualified for the Olympics if fence jumping had been a sport. As she pulled her other leg up and was about to lower herself to the other side she looked up at the back of the house, which she had been trying not to do. Nora met the stare of a man looking out her bedroom window. In the split second they looked at each other she saw his eyes wrinkle at the sides as he frowned furiously. She was terrified. It was the second time in three days she had seen that look. She never wanted to see "the face" again. She jumped down as fast as she could and ran through the yard, thankful there wasn't a dog in it. This yard wasn't fenced so she sprinted to the front of the house. Another deserted looking street. She ran several houses down looking at each one to see if anyone was home. She didn't see anything promising enough to warrant wasting the time. They would catch up soon. She looked back as she ran and saw one of them break around the house. It was the same man she had seen shooting the teenager behind the restaurant. The next time she looked back there were two men, and they were getting closer. The second man could have been one of the men from the hotel. Neither of them was dressed in a street gang manner. It looked more like business casual. She also spotted a gun in one of the men's waistbands. She continued to run as fast as she could, but her legs felt like jelly. Her lungs were burning and arms felt like lead. Palates classes didn't get one in good enough shape to sprint this distance. A black Taurus squealed around the corner and headed toward her. It must have been someone with the guys chasing her because when she glanced back to check the closing distance, they had slowed down and were grinning, but not with happiness. She turned and cut back between two houses, heading back to her own street. This house did have a fence, but the lock was hanging there, open. She opened it, jumped through, closed it, and locked it from the inside. Unfortunately, this yard did have a dog in it. A collie. It barked like crazy, scaring her to death. She kept moving toward the back, walking backwards, through the yard, but much more slowly than she would have liked. If she had run fast and offered it her back, the dog might have chased her down. The men were at the gate and started to climb it. The dog's owner stuck his head out the back door and began to yell at her. She screamed frantically for him to call the police. He didn't understand. He thought she was daring him to call the police on her. She screamed it again and pointed to the fence where two men were frozen on the top. The dog's owner finally looked around to his side where she had been pointing as one of the men jumped into the yard. The dog's owner stormed outside and grabbed one of the men chasing her. The other man on the fence jumped down. He looked at the two men fighting, took out his gun, and shot the dog's owner, as she screamed "No!" The dog ran toward the man trying to stand up after the skirmish. The man with the gun casually lifted his arm and shot the dog too. He didn't even flinch. Nora took off running again and no longer felt tired. She frantically climbed over the back fence and didn't look back even once. She didn't want to see the bullet before it hit her. She heard another shot but didn't feel it so she had no idea where it was intended to go. Surely someone would have heard the shot and called the police. It didn't matter to her. Even if they got here in a record four minutes, it would be three too late for her. She was on her last wind and could barely see through the tears streaming from her eyes. She hadn't started to cry until the man killed the dog. She had been shocked to see the man shot, but the dog brought forth uncontrollable emotion. This was really happening. Instead of running around the house and onto her street she began running down the back yards of her neighbor's houses. She did have some fences to contend with, but she tried to use anything around that would help, such as a tall root or lawn chair. She looked back as she went over the top of the fences. She didn't see anyone. She went back and forth randomly to the back yards of the houses on her street and the ones behind her. She avoided any yard with a dog, or where someone may be home. She would not be responsible for another innocent death if she could help it. She also didn't want barking to give her away. She didn't try to get a single person's attention even if they were obviously there. If the police hadn't already been called then she was on her own. She took a risk and went around to the front of one of the houses on her street. She could see her car in the driveway. One of the tires was flat. Great. Well at least she didn't have to worry about it being wired with a bomb. She was dealing with a penknife mentality rather than an explosives expert, but one without conscience. Up the block she saw the black Taurus turn onto the street. It was driving slowly. She went around behind the house again. She needed to get back to her house without being seen. Flat tire or not that car was her only way out. She quickly crossed over into a yard of the street behind her own. She made her way back peeking over fences and between houses to the street. She finally made it to her next-door neighbor's yard. The Fitzpatrick's were retired, but always had projects going on. They refinished furniture and periodically added on rooms to their house. They could fix anything. Thankfully they were on vacation visiting children and grandchildren in Kentucky for two weeks. Nora would never have gone into their garage if they had been home. She cared about them too much. She had a key to their house and garage on her key ring, which were still in her pocket from carrying out clothes to the car. She always locked her car doors, even when she was only going to be away for a minute. In Memphis, you lock it or look for it. She left her front door open, but locked the car. What an idiot she was. She let herself in the garage and looked out the window. She could see the black Taurus pass slowly down the street, with two men in the car. She looked around for a weapon to use if she needed it to get to her car. She found a thin, round piece of strong wood. It was probably the leg to a chair. She would try not to lose it or get it broken. Mr. and Mrs. Fitzpatrick would understand. She had her weapon in hand and was about to make a break for her car when she realized that someone would surely be watching it and she was walking into a trap with a chair leg. She locked the garage and ran to the back door of the house. Her hands were shaking from fatigue or fear, or both. She fumbled with the keys, which made so much noise she broke out in a cold sweat. After fooling with the lock for what seemed like an eternity it opened and she rushed in, barely able to keep herself from slamming the door. After bolting it behind her she got down low and crept to the front of the house. She peeked out the windows and didn't see anything. She thought about calling Allen but was afraid he would come right over and get himself killed. She decided to call Detective Whitman. He didn't believe anyone was interested in her. She'd just let him see for himself. Unfortunately she didn't have his card with her. She called directory assistance. Then called the precinct, blocking caller ID, and then was put on hold and transferred for no less than fifteen minutes. Finally she reached another detective who said Detective Whitman was out of the building. Nora was fairly mad by then.

"You find him, wherever he is and tell him that Nora Anderson, the witness to the Paulette's murder is being chased and the pursuers are at her house right now. I'm hiding someplace near the house but I've already been shot at and I have no idea how long I'll be safe here," she said.

"Tell me where you are so that we can protect you. I'm on my way right now," he said.

"I'm sorry, but I don't feel very confident in your ability to protect me right now. I'll come out as soon as I feel it's safe. Just get here fast," she said. Nora hung up the phone and realized that she hadn't given him her address. She was sure he could figure it out. She made her way back into the kitchen and opened the refrigerator to find a drink. Her mouth was so dry it felt as if it were lined with paper. Nothing but prune juice and condiments. She stood up to get a glass and turned to the sink to get water. She gulped down two glasses and then filled it a third time before returning to the floor. It was a good thing the Fitzpatrick's were such clean people. She was spending a lot of time on their floor. She crawled her way back into the living room, trying not to spill her water. The black car was in front of her house, parked. There was no one in it. Good, they would be in her house when the police got there. She called Allen and told him she had been delayed, but was fine. She also told him that she would get there as soon as she could. He said he had plenty of work to do but to hurry so they could spend some time together this evening. She hung up the phone and thought about how she wished she could just rush right over to get Allen that second. When she saw him she would have to tell him about what had happened today and he was going to be furious, especially since she just lied to him. If only the police would hurry and get there.

She didn't have to wait much longer before Detective Whitman pulled up along with two patrol cars. They got out and started to the front door quickly. From the Fitzpatrick's front, side window she couldn't see her front door or the porch so she just watched Detective Whitman as he walked through the yard. His fierce look broke into a grin. What in the world did he see? He took two more steps and reached out his hand. There wasn't a gun in it. He was grasping someone's hand. Her eyes wouldn't jump straight to the face that belonged to the hand. Instead they trailed up his arm, to his shoulder, to his neck and then came to the dark face and those eyes. Shock washed over her and she had to fight to breathe. Each breath was ragged and her throat ached to release sobs. Her only hope at being rescued was making pleasant conversation with a murderer. Not just any murderer, but the one who wanted her next. The patrolmen looked confused at first, but Detective Whitman seemed to be introducing them and they soon relaxed and began talking to each other. They all walked to the front of her house and she assumed they went in. They must have been inside for about fifteen minutes while her mind raced through the implications of what she had seen. It probably wouldn't go over well for her to just run up and accuse those men in front of the detective and the patrolmen. She would look like a ranting fool. The only chance she had would be to do what southern women had been doing to get their way with southern men for centuries. Play dumb. It wasn't her favorite way to handle things but it definitely had its place. She went around to the back door. The back yard was as clear as she expected, so she left and locked the door back before running around to the side opposite of her house and straight to her front yard. She was terrified with knees shaking but didn't stop until she was almost to her porch when Detective Whitman was coming out of her house. Nora decided she might be safe because the patrolmen obviously were not in on whatever was going on there. She wished she were in on what was going on there.

Hopefully they would hesitate before killing her in front of so many witnesses. He looked genuinely concerned about her and put his arm around her shoulders as he asked her to calm down and explain what happened. It took everything she had in her not to pull away from him. She took a few deep breaths like he told her to, which she really needed.

"I was in my house packing a few things when some men came in," she said.

"Was it these men here?" He asked.

"I don't know because I hid as they walked around the house until they were in the back. Then I ran out the back door. They chased me down the block but I was too scared to see their faces," she lied.

"You mean you didn't see anyone's face? How many men were there?" He asked.

"I'm not sure, more than two, probably fewer than five," she said.

"I can't believe you didn't see a single face when you were being chased outside during the day," he said. Nora could tell he was incredulous at her stupidity.

55

"Who are these men?" She asked. They looked at her suspiciously. They did not seem at all worried that she might accuse them. She was glad she hadn't.

"These are officers with the Vice Department. They came by to check out your house and to see if you were home so that they could ask you some questions," Detective Whitman said.

"Yes, we suspect that the killing you witnessed was connected to a drug deal gone bad. I'm Detective Spencer," said the man who was obviously the leader. "We need to ask you some questions so we can get this killer off the streets." He looked her straight in the eyes. These were the same cold eyes that had been haunting her. She couldn't believe the balls this guy had. She tried to look calm instead of the shock she felt. She met his stare and said,

"I can't talk about this right now. I'm really too shaken up to be any good to you at all. My car has a flat; could someone help me change it so I can go back to my hotel?" Nora could see she had come across as cool and confident. He seemed to look surprised and a little more relaxed. If he thought she wasn't afraid maybe he wouldn't try to find her again. Maybe he'd believe she didn't recognize him. She pulled her car keys out of her pocket to give them to the patrolman who stepped forward. Her hands were shaking so badly that the keys rattled loudly and she almost dropped them. Nora handed them off and quickly glanced at Spencer to see if he noticed. He had been looking at her hands and as his eyes met hers he frowned and then grinned. He knew. Detective Whitman took her hand and asked her if she would just answer their questions while a patrolman changed the tire. He was treating her like she was a child. She felt like one. She told him she just couldn't and broke into tears. Nora couldn't make herself cry, the tears were real. He took her inside to sit down while he told the Vice Officers that she would meet them tomorrow in his office. She told him it had to be after work, but not to tell them she was going to work. He looked at her funny but she explained they might not want to wait until five and show up at work. She convinced him she could get fired. He agreed and told them five. He said they'd been annoyed by the added delay. She watched them drive away from a window. Detective Whitman was telling her she shouldn't have run today. He said she should have called 911 and hidden.

"The vice guys must have just missed you. It's too bad they didn't get

56

here earlier," he said.

"I know you won't believe me," she said, "but they were the men who were after me." He laughed. She couldn't believe he had the nerve to laugh.

"You're right, I don't believe you. Why would you say that? I believe your house was searched and you were chased. You don't have to make up suspects. I know now I should have taken your fears more seriously. I'm sorry," he said.

"This is not some petty accusation because you didn't believe me. Not only were those the men that hunted me today, but Detective Spencer was the killer at Paulette's," she said.

"Do you think I'm crazy?" He spat out, incensed. "You described the killer as looking like a gang member. Detective Spencer doesn't look like a gang member. If you really think that's true then I'm not sure I can consider you as a competent witness," he said.

"Please deem me as an unreliable witness! But do it publicly so they will stop trying to get me. Look, I really am telling you the truth. I knew you wouldn't believe me but I had to tell you in case something happens to me. You have to check it out. Just don't forget," she said.

"If you have some proof of course I'll check it out right now. Do you?" He asked.

"No, if I did I would have given to you already. The only proofs I have are my eyes and my memory. I've read about how unreliable witnesses can be, but I promise you it was him. I wish I could forget, but I can't. Maybe he'll believe I didn't recognize him, but I doubt he'll take the chance." Even as she said the words she knew it was just wishful thinking. She saw the look of realization in his eyes. She hadn't fooled him.

"Look, Nora, I know it would easier for you if we dismissed you as a witness but then there would be no one to speak for that poor dead boy. Who can help Dedrick Ray seek justice besides you?" He said.

"I can't help anyone if I'm dead. Oh, God, I forgot to tell you; they shot some innocent man on the street behind me, and his dog. I tried to get away by going through his yard, but they shot him. Please send an ambulance in case it's not too late," she said. He called out side to a patrolman. She gave him an approximate location. Her tire was changed. Detective Whitman would only let her go if she gave him her hotel and room number. She told him she was staying in room 437 at the Crowne Plaza. Why should she tell him where she was staying when he was buddies with the killer? Or should she say killers. If he were much of a detective he would figure out she was staying with Allen anyway.

eight

Nora drove her car as fast as she could to get Allen. She had called him on her way so he was coming out as she drove up. He looked annoyed with her so she didn't tell him about the mess she'd just been in. They went straight to his apartment. Allen lived in a complex with many other young professionals. The buildings were fairly new with brick exteriors. There were large areas of grass, like mini parks where people walked, ran, and exercised their dogs. There were also several swimming pools and tennis courts. It was very open and well lit. This was one of the safest places she could think to be. Most people only lived there for a few years but the neighbors were fairly stable for an apartment complex. The crime rate was low because of good security and watchful neighbors. It made her a little angry that while those goons could run through her neighborhood unnoticed, brandishing weapons no less, they wouldn't have a chance here. She and Allen took a short walk, about ten minutes, and then went in to find some much needed dinner. She sat on the couch and told Allen about her afternoon while he listened and cooked. She could tell with each turn of events he was getting really pissed off. When Nora finished she just sat there and let the silence fill the room. Finally he spoke in what could only be described as a controlled rage.

"Do you have anything to add to your tale?"

"No," she said.

"Fine. Do you realize how stupid that was? If you don't give a damn about yourself at least consider how your being killed this afternoon would have affected me. Can you imagine the guilt I would have to live with, knowing that I was sitting in my office doing paperwork while you were fighting for your life? If you think so little of me then maybe we shouldn't be together. You obviously don't trust me," he said. She was expecting a lecture but it hit her like a blow.

"Allen, why would you think I don't trust you? I just didn't want to get you mixed up in all this. I could never forgive myself if you got hurt because of me," she said.

"Nora, you have no idea what a relationship is, do you? You can't just pick and chose what you share. You have to share the good and the

59

bad. You have to be able to trust that I'll be a help to you, rather than a hindrance," he said.

"I'm sorry Allen; I guess I didn't look at it that way," she said. "Do you really want to stop dating?" Her nose started to burn and tears started to fill her eyes. Damn it. The last thing she wanted to do was cry. She'd done entirely too much of that lately. Also, she didn't want Allen to say he wanted to keep dating because he felt sorry for her. She bent her head down to pick up a piece of mail off the floor so he couldn't see her face. She read the address as a distraction. It was Allen's address but someone else's name. It was addressed to Robert Cummings. He must have lived here before Allen. When he spoke it pulled her attention back to the present situation.

"I don't want to lose you, but you've changed a lot in the last few days. You used to come to me with your problems so we could work them out together. You always talked about how important it was to openly communicate and how that was why we were such a great couple. Now you sneak around and don't include me in decisions that affect your life. I need some time to think about this. Maybe we aren't such a good match if you ditch me at the first real stressful event" he said.

"Allen, I'm sorry, I wasn't thinking clearly. I just panicked..." she said. The phone was ringing. Nora wanted him to ignore it but he turned his back to her and answered it. He said a few words she couldn't hear. It irritated her that he was being so secretive, but she deserved it, didn't she? He turned around to hand her the phone. His face was filled with pity rather than anger. That was odd. She picked up the phone and said hello. She didn't say anything else for some time.

"Hello? Nora, are you still there?" Monica asked. "Hello." Finally she found her voice.

"Yes, I'm sorry...I can't believe this is really happening. Are you sure it was her that called? It was Helen?" Nora questioned.

"Yes, of course I'm sure. I wish I weren't," Monica said.

"Where did she say she wanted to meet me? Where was she when she called?" Nora asked.

"She wants you to meet her at the entrance to the zoo. It will be closed but she said she felt safe there. She wouldn't tell me where she was when she called. I tried to get her to meet you some place more public but she said she couldn't without drawing attention to herself. She said her face is badly bruised and swollen," Monica said.

"Did she go to the police?" Nora asked.

"No, she said she wouldn't because she didn't know who to trust. She's really scared, just like the rest of us are. I think she should come here and stay with us until all this is over" Monica said.

"Yes, that's a good idea. I'll have her call you from the road so you can give her directions to Pickwick. If she seems seriously hurt please take her to the hospital in Jackson," Nora said.

"I will. Take care and don't trust anyone you don't know. Promise?" Monica said.

"I won't. Thank you." Nora hung up and turned off the stove, dinner on the back burner, literally and figuratively. She asked Allen if he would go with her to the zoo. He said he would. They put their fight aside and headed to the zoo, after some snaking and backtracking on the way, so anyone following would get lost. Allen could be a fast driver and took corners faster than she thought was safe. This was one night she didn't say anything about it. The zoo entrance was mostly dark, with some light from the parking lot floodlights. It made the large statues of the animals at the entrance look eerie and malevolent. This was one of her favorite places to go during the day, and for a few evening events. But all the other times there had been spotlights on each animal to make it look bright and inviting. Now the shadows had changed everything. She didn't see Helen anywhere but it wouldn't have been safe for her to just be sitting on the curb in full view waiting for her sister. The zoo is connected to Overton Park, which is large and pretty, but can also be dangerous, even during the day. Nora's stomach was in knots with worry about her. She and Allen cautiously left the car and walked toward the evil looking animals. Nora called her name a few times. They were standing in between the two rows when Helen came out from behind the crocodile. Nora sucked in her breath at the sight of her. Helen grinned a little, then winced as her split lip pulled.

"Is it that bad?" She asked.

"Worse," Nora answered. Allen stepped forward.

"Are you okay? What happened?" He asked.

"I went to the grocery to get some things. On my way back out, through the parking lot, I was walking by a van. Just as I got up beside it the side door swung open and a man grabbed me and pulled me

61

inside. I was so surprised I didn't even really fight him. By the time I took in a breath, I was inside and the door was closed," she said.

"What did he look like?" Nora asked. She cringed.

"He was kind of short and almost bald. He had on dark pants and a yellow windbreaker. He looked... vicious," Helen said.

"What do you mean?" Nora asked.

"He snarled and glared at me, like this wasn't some random thing. He looked mad at me personally. Maybe this has nothing to do with you. Maybe this guy hates me for some crazy reason. Or maybe he was just some sick fuck who hates all women and I happened to be in the wrong place at the wrong time and this is just a coincidence," Helen said.

"I can't believe that," Nora said. "What happened after he got you inside?" Helen looked scared again and her eyes had a glassy look.

"He didn't ask me anything, didn't want anything that I could tell. He threw me down on the floor of the back. I jumped up and he started hitting me. He would growl like a beast if I wrestled myself away from him. I just kept thinking I was in a crowded parking lot and that if I could just get out I would be okay. I guess he was trying to beat me unconscious so he could drive away." Nora moved closer to her. Helen sat down on the concrete base of the elephant and Nora held her hand.

"I could feel myself getting weaker and was fighting back less. He let up some like it was some kind of game to him and he wasn't ready for it to be over. I had been hitting and kicking him every chance I got but it didn't seem to faze him. As I realized he was about to win I got furious. I was so mad that a thin metal van wall was all that stood between freedom and me. I freaked out. I threw myself at him and screamed louder than I ever have in my life. The sound of it scared me as much as it did him. The look on his face spurred me on. I must have caught someone's attention outside because there was a knock on the door and someone asked if we were all right. The man looked irritated. Then someone slid the door open. Hands pulled me out and tried to hold onto the man. He avoided the grabs and drove away as several other people came forward. A young sacker was helping me up as the van squealed out of the parking lot. I thanked the guy as I stumbled to my car, crying like some kind of loon. People asked if they could help me or call an ambulance or the police. All I wanted to do was get away," she said. Nora felt so guilty and sad and angry all at once. She knew this wasn't some weird coincidence. If she hadn't involved Helen, none of this would have happened.

"I'm so sorry. I should never have called you or asked you for help," Nora said.

"Don't be ridiculous. I'm fine. Just a few bruises and it's not your fault," Helen said.

"You are going to Pickwick to stay with Stephan and Monica," Nora said, not agreeing with Helen but unwilling to argue the point.

"This is one time we are in complete agreement. Where will you be?" Helen asked.

"You're not going to call me or try to get in touch with me in any way," Nora said.

"What? If you think…"

"Forget it. No more contact until this entire situation is over. Please don't argue with me about it. Surely you can see that it makes it more difficult for both of us," Nora said.

"I guess since you have Allen I'll agree, but I don't like it and Mom will freak out," Helen said.

Up to this point Allen had been an observer rather than a participant in this conversation. He usually was when it came to her family.

"I promise you, Helen, I don't plan to let her out of my sight. Not for one minute" Allen said. Great. Now she had a babysitter. Nora didn't need someone else to feel guilty about getting caught up in this mess. She and Allen helped Helen get settled in the car and watched her drive away.

They stood in the parking lot staring into the night, not wanting to break the silence, which was as close to peaceful as they had been in awhile. Finally Allen turned and looked at her. She was relieved to see the coldness had left his eyes.

"I understand why you left me out. I forgive you for it, but don't ever do it again. You're strong, but not invincible. No one is," he said.

"I won't," she said. Nora knew she should say more, should thank him for understanding. She couldn't. She was tired of explaining herself and being humble. It was tempting for her to slip into the role of the helpless female and let him handle everything. The problem was that no longer being in control of things didn't mean they didn't affect her anymore. There were too many things beyond her control right now. She had to hold on to what she could. He looked at Nora a little expectantly but saw the look of determination on her face and cut her some slack. He laughed at her and put his arm around her shoulders. She relaxed and leaned against him some as they walked to the car. He really was being much more understanding of her than she would have been of him, if the roles had been reversed.

"We need a plan. I don't intend to wait for the police to figure this out, or to be killed. That's assuming the police are not directly involved," she said.

"I think we have to assume the police are involved based on what happened this afternoon. Even if Whitman isn't, he probably won't do anything about the vice guys who are. I don't think you should talk to them anymore," Allen said. They jumped in the car and locked the doors so quickly it made them laugh at each other.

"There really is nothing funny about any of this," she said, smiling in spite of her horror of everything that had happened.

"I know, there really isn't," he said. They continued to smile and spontaneously break into laughter. She shook her head at how strange and inappropriate a person's response to stress can be. They decided to go back to Allen's apartment and eat dinner, even though it had certainly become cold. They didn't say much during the ride back. She thought they should have been discussing strategies but instead just she zoned out and couldn't seem to refocus. She was too tired, too stressed, and too hungry. However she did feel a bit more relaxed since her closest family and friends were out of harm's way.

Allen's parking lot was almost full. She considered that a good sign; most everyone was home. Lots of cars equaled lots of witnesses. There weren't many people out walking tonight, but that wasn't too surprising since it was chilly with a ten-mile an hour breeze. They quickly made it to his door and hopped around until he managed to get his keys out. Neither of them had on a real coat, just lightweight jackets they had hastily thrown on. After what seemed like an eternity he opened the door and they dashed into the warm, dark room. As soon as she was in she became disoriented because she usually wasn't running as she entered the apartment. But of course it usually wasn't completely dark either. She spun around quickly to get back to the light coming in from outside. Just then the door slammed. Nora stopped dead in her tracks. Cold dread crept up her spine and around the back of her neck. She tried to make herself calm down; it had to have been the wind that pulled the door closed harder than it was intended. She was trying to catch her breath when the light came on. She squinted against the attack to her retinas. But even that split second of looking told her that she and Allen were not alone.

nine

Nora opened her eyes again and let them get used to the light. There were four men in the room besides Allen. He was standing near the door, not having made it as far in the room since he opened the door and let her go first. He obviously wasn't the one who slammed the door as there was someone standing between him and the door. The man had a gun pointed at Allen's back. That was better than at his head, she guessed. The guy at the door and the two guys on the opposite side of the room were all wearing jeans and jackets. The man standing next to her had on a suit. It was actually quite a nice suit. He looked as if he should have been going to a downtown office building and carrying a briefcase instead of the big black 9 mm that was pointed at her. The guys in jeans looked vaguely familiar to her, but she couldn't be sure she recognized them from The Peabody or at her house. She had been much too afraid, and running, both times to remember faces for sure. She knew she had never seen the man in the suit. He was tall, about six foot four inches, and gorgeous. He could have walked straight out of a Calvin Klein underwear ad. He had dark brown hair and chiseled features with a strong, square jaw. He was well built and proportioned to his height. This made him seem huge, and terribly intimidating. It was obvious he worked out but wasn't so big that he looked bunched up in his suit. Nora looked around the room, slowly, taking everything in. She was desperately trying to think of a way out but also not making eye contact with suit man. He laughed and she turned and looked at him from the shock of the sound.

"I can't believe you're trying to figure a way out when you know we have you. They told me you were slippery. I just figured you were lucky," suit man said.

"What do you want?" Allen asked.

"What do you think I want?" Suit man asked Nora, ignoring Allen.

"We don't care about playing any games. Just take my wallet and her purse. I have some valuables around here, just take anything you want," Allen said. Evidently that was not the right thing to say because suit man got annoyed.

"You fucking idiot. Do I look like a common criminal? If I had wanted steal you blind I could have done it without your being home.

I'm not a thief, as you well know. This is a business transaction that will be very profitable for me. Not to mention pleasurable." He said, leering at her. Why did he keep looking at her when he answered Allen's questions? Allen was no small guy at six foot one inch tall. He also wasn't weak. Suit man dismissed him as if he were a mosquito. Allen looked nervous but was by no means cowering to these men. He should have constituted a threat, even if only a minor one since he wasn't armed. She knew Allen kept a gun, but it was in his bedroom. Nora knew many people in Memphis who kept guns in their homes, but they were usually in the bedroom. She assumed people were most afraid of the vulnerability of sleep. Allen asked suit man what they wanted again. Nora was beginning to wish he would just be quiet and stop irritating the man. It might make them act more quickly. She could really use some time to think of something to do. It would be easier if her every emotion weren't so readable on her face. What she needed was a poker face and a plan. That's all.

"I wouldn't suggest shooting that gun here," she said boldly.

"And why not Miss Anderson?" Suit man asked. The guys in jeans were all smiling, enjoying their work.

"In case you didn't realize, there are a lot of people around here and they would not only hear the shot but also my screams. Surely you are concerned about attracting so much attention," she said, with a little more bravado than was prudent. Wait, how did he know her name?

"Not at all," he said. "Enough of this. Let's get on with it." He wasn't talking to Allen or her this time. There wasn't any humor in his voice either. His teasing was over and now he was all business. The two guys across the room quickly moved toward them. One stood next to Nora, ready to grab her. The other walked to Allen and joined his buddy. She started toward Allen but the guy grabbed her and pinned her arms to her side. She tried to struggle but didn't get an inch. This guy's arm was like steel. Nora stopped fighting to save her strength for an opportune moment. She glanced toward Allen when she heard a grunt and some scuffling. He slowly slumped over and they let him fall to the ground. She screamed but only got out a second of the noise before a hand clamped down over her mouth. She started struggling anew, feeling she was suffocating. Nora tried as hard as she could to either bite the hand that covered her face or to make it as difficult as possible to hold her. All she wanted to do was get to Allen to help him.

She wasn't even sure what was wrong. Had they broken his neck, drugged him, or knocked him unconscious? As she struggled all she could think about was getting to him. It should have made her curious as to why this man was the only one trying to hold on to her when there were three other men in the room. She was unaware because of the single-mindedness of her goal. After several minutes she started slowing down her struggles. This was partially due to the fact that she was exhausted, but also because she was decidedly low on air. The man's hand covered all of her mouth and part of her nose. Nora felt as though she might black out at any minute. It was at once a tempting and repulsive thought. It would be a brief respite from the anguish she felt, but then she would be even more vulnerable than she was now, if that were possible. She tried to calm down and control her breathing. They could hear her struggling to pull air through her partially covered nostrils because they told the guy holding her to let her breathe. It was followed by accented jibes and comments having to do with how he woos his dates and his taste in sex. This was a game to these people. Her life was ending and they were teasing each other. She let her legs crumble beneath her. Fuck them. If they wanted her standing then they could hold her up. Nora was resting and breathing. She sneaked a look over at Allen. She couldn't tell if he was breathing or not. The men kept chatting like they were in a locker room rather than in someone's living room where they were most certainly not invited. She listened to their thick accents but could not tell the origin. Well, maybe she should have been happy they were talking because the next move would be to kill her too. She was sure they killed Allen first because they didn't want him to interfere with her and they knew she would not be able to help him. Nora hated she was so predictably weak. It became quiet in the room. She hadn't been paying attention but wallowing in self-pity. She looked up and they were all looking down at her. Suit man crouched down to talk to her like she was a spoiled child having a tantrum.

"We are leaving now and you are coming with us. You're a smart girl. How do you choose to go?" He asked slowly, like she was anything but a smart girl. Nora just sat there and looked at him like he wasn't speaking her language although his accent was definitely mid western American. What did he mean by 'how do you chose to go'? She was certain it was a trick question and was stumped as to how she should answer.

"Let me make it easier for you since you seem to be having trouble with that one. We can drug you and carry you out of here or you can walk out willingly. I warn you though. Don't think you can get away. I'll kill you before letting you escape. Remember, this is business for me. Nothing more. I have a reputation to protect and your life means nothing to me. Make up your mind quickly or I'll decide for you," suit man said. It was an easy decision for her.

"I'll go without fighting or running away. I have no desire to be drugged. Plus I wouldn't want you to have to carry me and Allen." She grasped at the thought that they had only drugged him, assumed that they had made his decision for him because of his size and strength. The cold smile on the suit man's face made her cringe.

"It would serve no purpose to carry him out. He is no longer a player in this game," he said.

"No..." she started to ask him to tell her he was lying, that what he said meant anything other than what she thought it meant.

"You'd better suck it up really fast or we'll see what's behind door number two. I have no patience for hysterical chicks so dry up or I'll put you out. I promise you won't like that hangover. It's worse than an all night fraternity party," he said. She did just what he told her to do. She wiped off her face and swallowed the sobs that were fighting to be released. She would be killed eventually. She had no doubt about that. At this point dying wasn't as scary to her as the way she might die and what would be done to her before it happened. This man had the power to make those decisions. He was in control now; there was no denying it. He probably wasn't completely cruel or he wouldn't have given her the option of how she wanted to leave. Maybe he was really just a businessman, of sorts, and was just providing a service, albeit a highly illegal one. She would do everything in her power not to provoke him. Even if she were only a job to him, he was potentially her lifeline. So when he stood up and extended his hand, she reached up and took it. She let him help her to her feet and stood beside him, even if she was a bit wobbly. Now was a good time to prove her obedience. Unfortunately, she had to ask to go to the bathroom.

"I know you aren't trying something already, are you?" He asked.

"No, I swear I have to go," she said. She looked him straight in the eyes and the honesty of her expression must have shown through

69

because he said okay. She turned around slowly, avoiding Allen's direction altogether. She couldn't do anything for him anymore. Nora knew he would want her to do whatever she had to not to die. She made her way slowly to the bathroom, not wanting to be tackled for a wrong move, stepped into the room, turned on the light and started to shut the door. Suit man stepped in. He no longer had his gun in his hand so it was hard to believe he wasn't just some executive breezing through the door.

"What?" She asked expectantly. She really had to go to the bathroom so she wished he would continue his lecture on his rules and her obedience later. He stood there and looked at her. Not just her eyes or even her face. He looked at her, up and down. As a woman, Nora knew what that look meant and it was not what she wanted. She had a funny feeling in the pit of her stomach, and it was fear.

"Please, just let me go to the bathroom really quickly. I promised you I wouldn't do anything and I won't," she asked, sounding more panicked than she wanted him to know.

"Go ahead," he said. He didn't move or take his eyes off her.

"Could you just turn around if you don't trust me enough to leave the room?"

"There is no trust between us. And no, I won't turn around. You'd better get used to my presence in everything you do. I'm sure we'll end up being quite close before the end," he said. The end. That didn't sound like this would just finish one day then life would go on, at least not for her. And she definitely didn't like the sound of 'quite close'. Well, what the hell was she supposed to do now? Wetting her pants didn't seem like a shameless resolution. If this prick got his jollies from seeing women pee then she would just have to be this evening's entertainment, wouldn't she?

"Fine," she said, hoping she sounded like it wouldn't bother her at all. She would just pretend she was in a crowded ladies room at a bar, like when she was in college. Many times there weren't doors on the stalls but no one ever thought anything about it. If you had to go badly enough... And she sure did. Of course, it had helped that they were drunk. She took a deep breath and undid her pants as quickly as she could and pulled them down as she was sitting. Nora didn't want him to get any joy from anticipation like she was stripping for his pleasure or anything. She knew he couldn't see anything while she was sitting down because she let her shirt cover most of her lap. She tried to ignore him but could feel his stare. She forced herself to relax. It was really hard but she didn't want to be half naked in front of this man for another second. Finally she started to go and forced it to go as quickly as possible. She knew there should be no shame in performing bodily functions but her face was hot with embarrassment. She was humiliated. This wasn't arousing for him; it was another way to intimidate her. She quickly wiped, pulled up her pants, flushed, and went over to wash her hands, trying to pretend it meant nothing to her. Nora thought she was doing well until she looked in the mirror. Her face was bright red. He caught her eye in the reflection and smiled. She could have killed him at that moment. But she wouldn't give him any excuse to drug her. She walked out into the living room but stopped when he grabbed her arm. She turned to face him.

"I'm going to blindfold you, and then we're going to walk out that door and to the car. I'm your only way out of here alive. If you hold on to my arm, and don't let go, you'll live. If you take off the blindfold or let go of me then we'll shoot you on the spot. We will safely surround you so don't worry about anyone trying to snatch you from my arm. Of course if they do, you'll be dead," he said. She just nodded. She couldn't speak, could barely move. She had to completely trust these people who wanted to kill her. They tied the blindfold around her head. It wasn't like Pin-the-Tail-on-the-Donkey as a child when you could see the ground through the bottom of the bandanna. She couldn't see anything. It was so disorienting not being able to see that holding on to suit man's arm was not the problem she thought it would be. Nora thought she would be repulsed by his touch, but honestly she needed him to be able to do anything. She was so alone and afraid that he offered security on some level. It was a little like an abused child seeking out the abusive parent for comforting after being beaten. Except in her case the beating hadn't come yet. Yet.

ten

The cold night air made her more alert. Nora wanted to run until she couldn't take another step. She didn't see Allen as they left since her eyes were covered, but she felt an overwhelming sadness as they passed where she knew he had been lying on the floor. She realized this was probably her best, if not only chance to escape, but it wasn't much of a chance. She didn't doubt they would kill her. She couldn't run if she couldn't see and they would shoot her if she even reached toward the blindfold. So she took another deep breath and held on to suit man tighter. Nora didn't want to trip and lose her hold on his arm. It would be just her luck to get shot for being a klutz. He reached over and patted her hand like an affectionate lover. They must have passed some people because she heard voices and they started to walk faster. Some guy asked what was going on. No one from Nora's entourage said a word, just kept walking. A couple of voices came from behind them. It sounded like a large group of people but she couldn't be sure.
"Hey, lady, you okay?"
"Hey man, let go of her."
"What the hell you think you're doing?"
The good Samaritans seemed to be following Nora's group, but from a distance. They sounded like they may have been drunk. She was tempted to scream. It might be her only chance. Suit man must have read her thoughts because in a very low voice he said"...only if you want to get them killed." Nora knew she wouldn't utter a word or sound. While she might risk herself, she wouldn't risk these guys just trying to be chivalrous. They sounded like they might be getting closer and a bit more rowdy. Nora wasn't sure what happened because she couldn't see and no one from her group said a word, but she assumed a few members of their group stopped to show the drunk guys the latest in automatic weapons because they became very quiet for a second and then said things like "shit man, awe, hell no. We got no problem here." And then they were gone. She was glad they got away. Maybe they would call the police. It would be nice if someone at least knew she had been kidnapped and was maybe looking for her. Not that they would find her. Nora had a feeling these guys had taken people before

and were probably good at it.

She was handed into a vehicle of some kind. She had to step up so it was probably an SUV or a van. It smelled new. Someone put a seatbelt on her, which she found amusing. Why protect her from harm in a traffic accident if they planned to kill her, of which she was certain they did. The vehicle was moving along at what felt like a normal pace. She guessed they didn't want to attract attention from police. Not being able to see, along with not eating dinner, was making her a little car sick. She had no idea how long they were in the car. It seemed like hours. No one spoke the entire time. No radio was on. She was so miserable time would have passed slowly for her anyway. Nora had read where some captives counted in their heads to figure out how far away they'd been taken. She wasn't dedicated enough to the task of getting away because all of her energy was focused on not throwing up. For all she knew, they could have been driving in circles. She finally spoke up and asked whoever was sitting beside her, she assumed suit man, if he would roll down her window a little.

"Why, you planning on jumping out?" He laughed. It was suit man.

"I'm a little nauseated right now. I haven't eaten in awhile and not being able to see is making me a little dizzy," she explained. He sighed deeply, then she heard the window come down at the same time she felt the cool air rush in. She turned her head toward it and lifted her nose up just the way a dog does. She started to feel a little better. She didn't even mind the sting of the cold. After some time they slowed down and drove over some uneven ground she assumed was either a drive way or a parking lot. They parked and men got out, opening and closing doors. Nora just sat there until she was told to move over to the door. She was going to be the model of obedience and bide her time until she had a solid plan. By that time they would trust her, if only just a little. Maybe that would be enough.

"Same drill as before. You've been a good girl so far. Don't fuck it up now. Come on, slowly" he said as he helped her out of the vehicle. She didn't respond because she knew talking was out. Nora grabbed his arm and walked. She was on a date stroll with her boyfriend, the psychopath. How cute.

eleven

She was led through what seemed to be a series of rooms. Nora could smell the faint odor of cleaning products and cigars. Then she walked across floors that were maybe wood with some thick area rugs. It was difficult not to stumble over the uneven surfaces while blindfolded. Finally they stopped and he let go of her arm. He took off the blindfold. Her eyes had to adjust to the light even though it wasn't very bright. She looked around. The floor was carpeted in a neutral, tan-like color. The walls were cream colored. There were no pictures on the walls. There were no windows, but there was a skylight. At least she would be able to tell if it was day or night. There was a bed in the room. It seemed to be queen sized, without headboard, just on a frame. There was also a small wooden table, more the size of a nightstand. There was no other furniture in the room. The bed had sheets on it, but no blankets or pillows. Not exactly comfortable, but better than it could be, all things considered. She stood there waiting for suit man to start in with the rules again. He looked at her for a minute.

"Sit down" he said as he motioned to the bed. She only hesitated a second before doing what he said. She could do this. He stood right in front of her so that she had to look up at him. It was an uncomfortable position and one of complete subservience.

"Let me explain how things work. You will do everything I say-immediately. You will not leave this room unless you are with me. No exceptions. You will not even try to open the door. If you even touch the door knob, you will be punished." He walked to the door without looking back, opened it, and left. She sat there for a minute fighting the urge to panic. He hadn't said he would come back much less when. She could rot in this room and no one would know or care. She should have been happy they were leaving her alone. Things could have been much worse. She suspected it wouldn't take much effort to get what they wanted from her. And what could they want from her anyway? Then they would kill her. As much as she believed all that to be true, she still couldn't help feeling afraid of being alone. Nora needed to be doing something to keep her mind on a more productive tract. She started looking around the room for possible places to hide or escape. A weapon was out since the only things available were the small table and the bed frame. She would be a formidable opponent swinging a six-foot long metal rung from a bed frame. Actually she would probably hurt herself more than anyone else. The table could be used, but only as a last resort. There was no chance of her going out without a nasty fight. She had little experience in fighting. That certainly would not have fallen in the realm of "lady-like" which was her mother's mantra while she was growing up. Even so, her survival instincts were building up and growing so that she hoped she wouldn't be an easy kill. There were no windows, one door that was forbidden, and a skylight that was at least twelve feet from the ground. The lack of furniture prevented any climbing up to the skylight, which would not have been easy to break anyway. As tempting as it was to try the door, she decided she would continue with her original plan to feign obedience. They would be expecting her to try that now. Later, maybe they would relax. She was soon tired of pacing the floor, but hesitated before sitting again. The bed itself was scary to her. It represented possibilities she didn't want to consider. She was somewhere alone, with several men at least. Nora was sure they weren't bound by the same social rules of conduct to which she was accustomed. Not only that, but they definitely didn't value her life or happiness at all. Suit man had already made his intentions clear. In theory she could tell herself that if she had to face the possibility of being raped it was horrible and she would fight with everything she had, but she would still have her life. Being killed should be the scariest possibility. But it wasn't. Dead is dead. No more pain. It's over. Being raped or tortured might be worse because the fear would never go away. None of the possibilities were pleasant.

She sat down on the floor in the corner and rested her arms and head on her knees. She tried to make her mind go blank. It didn't work but she started to relax. Exhaustion took over and she lay down on her side, curling into a ball. She felt like her eyes had just been closed for a few minutes when the door opened. The click from the lock had awakened her, so her eyes were open before the door opened. Suit man stepped in and looked at the empty bed and scanned the room looking until he saw her. The look in his eyes was relief. Gotcha. It gave her great pleasure to have caused him even a second of panic. That troubled look was much easier to bear than the arrogant look he had now. He had taken in the fact that she had been asleep since she was still lying on her side. Nora resisted the urge to scramble up and cower in the corner. She forced herself to slowly sit up as if she had not another care in the world. He started grinning, having quickly gotten over his shock at not seeing his hostage.

"If you think sleeping on the floor will prevent me from coming to you when I decide to, you're either naive or stupid," he said. He was right and she felt foolish.

"I don't know what you are taking about," she said.

"I think you do," he said. She didn't respond and he let the silence stretch for several minutes while he looked at her. She was sure it was another way to intimidate her, and it worked. She had the undeniable urge to squirm, which she did but without uttering a sound.

"Do you need to go to the restroom again?" he asked with a leering grin. The memory of the last time made her face hot with embarrassment. She was furious but kept reminding herself of the plan. Nora would be submissive if it killed her.

"No, thank you," she answered quietly. Luckily she really didn't have to go since she hadn't had anything to eat or drink recently. He looked a little disappointed that she wasn't going to argue with him. Good. Nora really needed food and water or she would become progressively weaker, which was not part of her plan. Asking for these things would pose two problems for her. One is that she would have to go to the restroom eventually and repeat an incident she would rather forget forever. The second problem was that she would have to request those things. The bastard was going to make her beg for food and water. It hurt her pride to even consider asking him for anything. And what if he refused? There was no alternative. He looked at her a little expectantly and then turned to leave.

"Wait!" She said, a little louder than intended. He turned around smiling, a man who must love his work. She couldn't remember having seen anyone smile so often.

"Could I please have some water, and maybe something to eat?" She said. There, she'd done it.

"And what do I get in return for those favors?" He asked, grinning like the arrogant fool he was.

"Only my gratitude for not letting me starve to death while you hold me against my will. And if you want anything at all from me you had better take that because that's all you'll ever get- willingly!" She answered. So much for maintaining polite aloofness. The man infuriated her. She should have never asked for a thing.

"When you think of a better offer let me know. There are many things I want from you and gratitude is not one of them. Until then I'll set your schedule as I see fit." He paused for a moment to see if she had anything to add to her previous performance. She bit her lip so her hostile reply could not escape. He left and she was glad to see him go.

After what must have been hours, as evidenced by daylight, she started replaying the conversation, if one could call it that, in her head. She should have asked when he would be coming back. If she could just stifle her temper and act more meager she could probably make more progress. Maybe she could get him in a casual conversation and find some information, anything. Some little hint might prove useful later. So far the closest they had come to conversation was barely veiled innuendo that was far from casual. Nora was a smart girl with more than a modicum of common sense. She'd never had any problems with maintaining self-control so it amazed her that she couldn't get control of herself now. She had actually been accused of being a control freak, but only by jealous friends or malicious ex-boyfriends. Her mind continued to wander through the 'could-haves' and 'should-haves' until she'd finally had enough. She began pacing around the room. It was light outside and bright. She couldn't see anything but clear sky. The idea of a bright beautiful day made her even more depressed. She imagined all the people walking down the sidewalk toward the hospital, laughing, and talking. Their day marched on, as they were blissfully unaware of her suffering. She wished she could go back to her ordinary life with no excitement or traumas. She doubted very seriously it could ever be that way again. Even if some miracle happened and she was rescued this very minute she didn't believe she would ever be the same. It does something to a person to be hunted, captured, and contained.

Nora had a headache that was from stress, low blood sugar, or dehydration. It would be a hard call to decide which was the more pressing problem. She lay down on the bed and tried to relax. Generally she found it possible to ignore many types of pain, but a headache was not one of them. Deep breathing and relaxing made it not so unbearable. She must have fallen asleep again because when she woke up the shadows in the room were very different, probably late afternoon. It was so silent. She listened for any sound. Was anyone there at all? Why could she not even here a car door or siren or television or barking dog or anything. Nora felt completely alone in the world. Thank God for the skylight or she would have been much more disoriented. Time rolled on and she stayed in a stupor of drifting in and out of light sleep and trying not to think about anything. It was beginning to get dark again. Could the whole day really have passed? She was just lying there spaced out looking at the sky when the door clicked again. She sat up quickly and pressed her back against the wall with her legs curled up under her. It was a defensive position but she couldn't help it. The door pushed open and suit man walked in. She tried to look out in the hall past him but saw only another bare wall. He closed the door. He was carrying a glass of water. She hadn't even allowed herself to think about how thirsty she was. Her tongue felt gluey and had a terrible taste. Maybe he would find her breath offensive and let her brush her teeth. She didn't want to make herself more appealing but would have taken the chance to have a clean mouth again. It was very demoralizing to be dirty. He walked over to the bed and sat down. She was much more interested in the glass he was holding than the risk he represented.

"It's time to get down to business. I know you want this water but you'll have to earn it." For once he looked serious and was not flirting. She just looked at him. Nora couldn't trust herself to speak or she might start crying.

"We'll make this easy to start. If you hadn't been so stubborn you wouldn't be in such bad shape right now. Maybe this was the entire lesson you needed. I'm sure you can now see the wisdom in being cooperative." She was sure he could see the unshed tears as she nodded her head. She had no thoughts or plans of rebellion. It was scary how quickly one's body focuses on the basics. The mind was no longer leading.

"Tell me about your employer," he asked.

"Mercy Hospital," she answered, guilelessly. Nora was glad he asked something easy because she was having trouble staying in control. He looked at her strangely.

"I know you're a nurse at the hospital, but that was not the employment I was referring to. I want to know your connection to this event," he paused expectantly.

"I'm not sure what you mean?" She asked.

"What do you do for your father's company? How are you involved?" He was beginning to be irritated. If she hadn't been so confused and weak she would have enjoyed his frustration. He seemed to be a man accustomed to getting exactly what he wanted.

"I promise you I don't work for anyone other than the hospital. I'm involved with the shooting only because I saw a small part of it and I don't have a clue what is going on. Everything is just out of control. I was at the restaurant where that man was shot. That's all I know. I was just at the wrong place at the wrong time. This doesn't have anything to do with my father or his business." Tears were slowly but steadily falling down her face. She wasn't sobbing but was barely managing to hold it together. Suit man was frowning at her like she should go on to the better explanation but it was all she had.

"There's more to all this, I'm sure. I may be a fool but I believe that you haven't put it all together," he sighed.

"I don't know anything and I don't want to. Just let me go and I will never give this another thought much less tell anyone. I don't even care anymore. Not about the kid whose face was blown off or the man who did it. It isn't my problem." She was beginning to rant. Nora wiped at the tears and sniffled. She was losing more fluids. Great. At this rate she would be dried up like a potato chip. Now she really felt sorry for herself.

"It's okay. We'll talk about this some more- I can't let you go until we do. Let me use some assistance while we talk and make sense of this whole thing." He was speaking very gently, like men do when women begin to come unraveled. He was doing something she had never seen him do before. He was being compassionate. He took his thumb and gently wiped the latest tear from her cheek. He put his arm around her shoulder and she leaned against him. It felt very natural and comforting. He pulled her closer and she buried her face in his neck. He was so warm and smelled great. They just sat like that for a few minutes. She knew she shouldn't trust him but was enjoying the feel of another person and the comfort of not being alone. He gently pushed her back until she was sitting on her own, but he was still close. Then he handed her the water. She started to drink quickly, like he might take it away.

"Slowly, slow down or you'll just throw it up," he said. He was right so she relaxed and paused in between swallows. She felt warmth spread through her body like a wilted plant finally receiving rain. She hadn't really been paying attention to everything he said because the "with assistance" part did not sink in until he continued to explain it.

"I can give you a little medication that will help you to relax so you can answer all my questions without analyzing the answers first. This will help us get down to the information I need and get you home faster," he said.

"I told you everything I know. I don't want to be drugged. What if it makes me confused and I say something incorrect. I don't want to die, especially over an error of information while I'm out of it." Nora was beginning to panic. He could sense this and began to slowly run his hand up and down her arm, softly. It had a very calming effect. Then he spoke carefully.

"I know you want to leave, and you will. I believe you don't have any active involvement in this...situation, but I can't complete this business and send you home until I'm sure I know everything you know. I'm discussing this with you first because I don't want you to be scared. I like you but there is no choice this time. It will not be anything psychedelic or addictive like they show on TV. It's just a very mild tranquilizer to make you calm enough to remember and tell me everything, not just what you think I'm asking for. It will make you a little drowsy but you shouldn't even fall asleep. It will only last an hour or so. I want you to be okay with this for two reasons. One is I don't want to upset you any more than is necessary. The second is it will be faster and easier for you and me if you are not fighting the medication. This shouldn't be a problem since you have already decided to tell me what you know. This would only be a problem for someone who was hiding things from me." He started to pull away from her. Nora didn't want to feel alone again. She put her hand on his arm and looked at his face, deep into his eyes to see if anything was there that didn't ring true. He looked right back at her without hesitation or guile. She was sure she was a fool to trust a hired killer and kidnapper, but what do you have left when you can't trust your own judgment? It was a chance to prove she didn't know anything and maybe he would do as he said and let her go. Really there wasn't much of a choice to make since he would do it anyway, but she sensed it would make a difference to him if she had to be forced. She needed him to continue to be compassionate with her. She wasn't ready to be his adversary again. He was all she had right now, controlling her whole world. He could see her sorting it all out and patiently waited for her to answer.

"I'm really scared of this, but I want you to believe me. I'm telling you the truth. I'm past any kind of rebellion. I don't think you'll find out anything but you can try if you believe it might work. I'll only go along with it if you do it and don't leave me for a minute. I trust you, but no one else," she said.

"I swear I won't leave you for a minute. As soon as it's over you can have a shower and some food. I can't let you eat now because it might make you nauseated when I give you the medicine," he said. She understood that. She didn't want to have a stomach full of food when she was about to be sedated. What if she vomited and couldn't sit or roll over? She would choke. She nodded weakly that she agreed with his plan. He stood up and left the room saying he would be back in a minute, for her to get comfortable. He wasn't gone long enough to prepare anything he brought back with him, or for her to have second thoughts. He must have known or at least strongly suspected it would come to this. There was someone else with him when he entered the room. He called the man Jake but she was sure it wasn't his real name. Nora was nervous about having someone she didn't know or trust in the room when she wouldn't be able to defend herself. Suit man could see she was looking at Jake suspiciously and quickly explained his presence.

"I might need some help if you had a reaction to the medication. Also, he can record what you say so that I can just focus on you. I don't want to let go of you for a second," he said. Then he whispered softly in her ear, adding, "Don't be worried that Jake may do anything... inappropriate to you. I want you for myself, when you are ready to admit you want me too. I can wait. I don't have to force women when I want sex. A willing and eager partner excites me."

A flame ignited in her body and the passion had to have shown in her face. She hated to admit it but she was sexually attracted to him. There was something in the power he held over her. She fought those feelings because she was still having a very hard time reconciling the fact that this kind, compassionate, sexy man was the same asshole who abducted her and allowed or even ordered Allen to be killed. When she began to think in that direction she became anxious about trusting him. So she tried to stop those thoughts because at that moment they were counterproductive. Nora had no choice. She didn't have time to dwell on those confusing and conflicting feelings because they were ready to start. There was a tray set up and sitting on the small table. There were several vials on the tray. They were too far away for her to see. She hoped they had epinephrine in case she was allergic to whatever they were giving her. She tried not to think about that. She was detaching herself so she could watch as if this was all happening to someone else. They moved quickly and professionally. It was obvious they had medical training and experience. She was curious about what they were giving her but did not ask because she didn't really want to know. If she knew what name and class she would remember all the possible side effects and just become more anxious, if that were possible. He prepared her arm just as she would have done if she were starting an IV and with a slight sting had it perfectly placed in a vein. That was something that would have required practice because her veins were quite small. His technique was such that she wasn't overly concerned about infection or contamination. Everything came straight out of sterile packaging and looked as if it came straight off the hospital central supply shelf. They flushed the new line with saline and then slowly pushed a small amount of clear yellow fluid into her vein. Nora felt its effects almost immediately. Her skin felt flushed and her head felt as though it was floating. Then she started to feel a tinge of nausea. A glass of water on an empty stomach did not combine well with the floating feeling. She told him and he picked up another vial and injected a bit of it. It worked because she felt better although much more drowsy. She felt as though her head and mind were a thousand miles away from her body and the men in her small, almost empty room. Her thoughts wandered wildly and she could hear herself start to speak but didn't understand why she was speaking or what she was saying. Everything got blurry in her mind after that. It wasn't unpleasant that she could remember; just not clear enough to focus on any one thought. She did have a sense of time passing, though how much was illusive. She must have slept because after some time she woke up feeling very groggy. The first thing she noticed was that someone was beside her. He could tell she was waking up because he started petting her arm again. She tried to open her eyes but they wouldn't stay open. She drifted off a bit more then was able to really wake up but still had some residual drug effect. She smiled at him and asked how she did. Her speech was a bit slurred and her smile looked more like a silly, lopsided grin but she was blissfully unaware. She still felt sleepy but was able to fight it.

"You did great. You were very open and gave me an answer to every question. It was worth the effort," he answered. She reached up and touched the bandage where the IV had been.

"What did you find out?" She asked. Nora was curious about what she knew that he would be interested in. She didn't really know anything, did she? She hoped she didn't give the wrong impression.

"If you don't know then I am not going to tell you. With knowledge comes considerable burden. I wouldn't be doing you any favors," he answered. She would accept that for now because she was much too spacey to care.

"How about a shower? You can eat when you get out," he offered.

"Do I smell that bad?" She quipped, drunkenly. Before he had a chance to say anything she answered.

"I would love to take a shower, and eat."

"Good, and you don't smell bad but I know you'd be more comfortable." He got up and walked to the door.

"I'll be back in a minute," he said. Her mind refused to acknowledge any warnings. She didn't care about the risk she may have been taking. It couldn't be worse than throwing his consideration back in his face and his leaving her there to rot. That had taken her nowhere so far. They had even embraced and it had not spun out of control. He saw that this was all just a mistake and she was innocent of all his suspicions. Nora didn't even want to speculate about what was really going on. The time had come to take care of herself. All in all she was feeling much more optimistic about the whole situation when he came back in. It must have shown on her face because he smiled at her and she smiled back.

"Are you ready?" He asked.

"Absolutely," she answered, as she stood, not a little unsteadily. She bent over to grab the bed to gain her balance and then was fine. He walked toward her and put both hands on her shoulders. She looked up at his face and was a bit dizzy again. His grip tightened just slightly.

Her stomach protested with instant queasiness. She swallowed and fought the urge to gag. Dizziness had always made her nauseated and she really needed to eat. Nora put as calm an expression on her face as possible. She didn't want him to think it was his proximity that was making her sick. She couldn't afford to start over making peace with him at this point. Not to mention that his touch made her feel quite tingly. His smile warmed a few degrees. Lord, he was gorgeous. He looked like a god.

"I don't want to scare you again but I have to put a blind fold on you to go to the other room. I have to maintain the security of this location and you don't want to have more knowledge than we could afford to let you leave with, do you?" He said gently.

"No, I definitely do not. Please blindfold me. I don't want to know anything except when I can go free," she answered. He pulled the blindfold out of his pocket. He had long ago lost the suit. He had on jeans and white button down shirt. His top button was undone and his sleeves were rolled up. There was mascara on his collar where she had buried her face while was crying. She must look a mess. She hadn't brushed her hair or anything. Nora couldn't believe she was worrying about her appearance when she had been abducted. It's not like she was on a date or anything. When the blindfold was secure he led her across the room and through the doorway. She didn't hear a sound. They had to be the only ones there. They didn't go far before they turned through another doorway and she was no longer walking on carpet. Nora stopped and he closed the door. He took off the blindfold and she looked around the room. It was small and typical of a guest bathroom. A toilet, vanity, and shower stall were compacted into a space no bigger than her walk-in closet at home. There were two towels folded on the vanity with a washcloth folded on top. There was nothing on any of the walls and only a cheap bath mat on the floor. She just stood there not sure where to start but wanting to badly. She hated feeling so awkward and wished he would just show her where everything was and leave so she could get on with it.

"Should I just put these same clothes back on when I get out? I didn't pack a bag or anything," she said, a little embarrassed, though mostly sarcastic. Although why she should be embarrassed was a mystery. He knew more than anyone why she didn't have any clothes to change into. She was starting to feel a little irritable.

84

"I have something for you to put on. It isn't exactly glamorous but it's clean. You can just wear it until I can have the clothes you have on cleaned. Go ahead and get undressed. I know from the look on your face that you want me to go but I can't. I still have security to consider. I would be protecting you as much as guarding you," he said. Nora started to protest but he shushed her, then helped her sit down on the closed toilet seat. He took off her running shoes and socks. This was much different than the last time they were in a bathroom together. She didn't argue. She just didn't have the strength. Nora unbuttoned her pants and stood up to slip them off. He stood beside her and put his hand on the small of her back for support as she slipped her feet out of each leg. She unbuttoned her blouse and slipped it off. He helped her pull the sleeves off. She didn't think she could have done it if he had just been standing there, watching her. His helping prevented her from feeling like she was on display. He reached around and unhooked her bra. She bent over and stepped out of her panties. He took a step toward the shower, opened the door, and started the water while still holding on to one of her arms. When it was warm he turned to help her in, except hearing the water reminded her of the need to urinate again.

"Um, I need to use the restroom before I get in" she said, tentatively. Nora wasn't sure if the leering jerk would be back. He continued to hold her arm, and moved away from the shower. After she was seated he turned to check the water temperature again and put a washcloth in the shower, allowing her a moment of privacy. Ok, so not the jerk. Who is this guy? The flush seemed to be his cue to turn around and help her up. She really could have stood up by herself but wasn't going to break the peace over solicitous behavior. Nora stepped into the perfectly warm stream of water.

"Call if you need me, okay?"

"I don't know your name," she said.

"You can call me Adam." She knew it wasn't his real name but remembered what he said about knowing too much and how dangerous it could be for her. She looked at him for a second, then closed the shower door. It was clear glass but the view would be distorted because of the steam and water drops clinging to it. She was too relieved to care if he did watch her. The water felt so good. She lathered every inch of herself and rinsed carefully, leaning against the wall a little to stay steady. There was a razor so she shaved her legs and underarms. It felt so good to be back to normal, at least in the way of personal hygiene. She opened her mouth and drank some water after rinsing her face. She opened her eyes and saw Adam watching. Up to that point she had been so intent on getting clean, and still a bit fuzzy headed, that she hadn't thought about his watching her every move. Even through the small amount of distortion she could see his eyes clearly enough to recognize lust. His gaze was no longer concerned and kind. He looked every bit the predator she'd met in Allen's apartment. And she felt like prey. She was scared. But if she were honest with herself, fear wasn't all she was feeling. Nora watched him stare. He didn't hide his hunger from her. After what felt like minutes, but was probably only seconds, his eyes left hers and went to the rest of her body. It made her self-conscious. He had to have seen all of it while she was washing, touching herself. Now he wanted her to watch him look. She suddenly wanted to cover up, but willed herself to stand still for the count of three, then slowly turned around to rinse one last time. Her breathing was fast and she was sure her heart rate was too. She knew why she was scared of him. That was good sense. What she didn't understand was why he turned her on too. She turned off the water and opened the door. Adam was waiting with a towel. His eyes still devoured her body, but he smiled gently as he came to her and helped wrap her hair up. Then he got a second towel and started wiping off her body. She tried to take the towel to do it herself, having hit her limit of humiliation. Adam wrapped it around her, pinning her arms by her side. He pulled her in close, reached down, and barely bit her ear lobe. Her breath caught. He spoke softly in her ear, his warm breath making goose bumps appear down her arms.

"Nora, don't start fighting me now. Remember the rules. Do you want us to stay friends?" He asked.

"Yes," she breathed out, barely able to make sound.

"Good girl. Now let me do what I want to help you. Don't fight me." All she could do was nod. Adam continued with drying and she let him. He finished quickly and was more business-like than sensual, which was good. Nora had so many conflicting emotions going on she was in danger of either exploding or crying, neither of which she wanted to do. Maintain some control, Anderson, she thought. Her skin was pink from the heat of the water and the friction of the towel. She felt great, if not a bit dizzy. He opened new toothpaste and a toothbrush then gave them to her. After brushing thoroughly she rubbed lotion on her hands, arms, legs, and face while Adam rubbed lotion on her back. He wasn't as efficient with his application, but his felt better. She took her hair out of the towel and quickly brushed the tangles out. She tried to be as quick as possible because if she didn't eat soon she would throw up. That would be unacceptable considering she had just managed to get her mouth clean. She put on deodorant and slipped on the t-shirt and running shorts Adam handed her. They were much too big but she didn't complain. Nora felt a little too free with the loose clothing and no underclothes. It was probably a good sign that he didn't have a supply of women's underclothes hanging around.

"Ready?" He asked.

"Yes, thank you," she said. He put the blindfold back on and took her back. She settled on the bed while he went to get dinner. There was no thought of anything but the upcoming meal. He was back within a few minutes carrying a tray. On it was a bottle of wine, carafe of water, bread, cheese, and fruit. It looked wonderful.

"I don't cook but this should do the trick."

"It looks divine," she said. He poured water into a glass and handed it to her. She drank it all. Her stomach was growling audibly. Adam moved the table closer to her so she could reach the bread. He sliced cheese and opened the wine while they chatted about their favorite wines and cheeses. He had chosen a nice red for them, which happened to be one of her favorites. The wine went to her head quickly so she felt warm and a little giddy. She briefly hoped the alcohol wouldn't be too much when mixed with the medication, which was mostly gone anyway. He sliced an apple and handed her pieces. She would have sworn it was the best meal she had ever had. Adam was using a sharp knife and did the entire cutting for them both. An unspoken rule existed that she was not to get near it and she didn't. Nora didn't want to be the one to spoil the detente. Deep inside she knew this wouldn't work for long but so much bad had happened she was willing to ignore a lot to laugh and talk, if only for a little while. She stopped looking, at least consciously, for a way to escape. She was relaxed, full, happy and more than a little drunk. Her face must have told all of that. Adam looked at her and smiled. He was so charming when he wanted to be. It didn't take long for her stomach to feel content. Although it was tempting to overeat, she didn't want to feel sick. It had already happened too much lately. Plus, there shouldn't be any concerns about being fed now. Adam had to establish his dominance over her in the beginning in case she had the information he wanted. Her brain was too giddy to follow through on any of these thoughts or to draw any meaningful conclusions. Nora had stopped eating and drinking wine but was still sipping some water. Adam was telling her about the history of the wine they were drinking and his trip to visit the vineyard in California. He seemed very knowledgeable on the subject. She had to focus to follow what he was saying and to respond intelligently. He didn't seem the least bit drunk but was so much more relaxed and, well, human than he had been before. She found herself watching his mouth as he spoke. His lips were soft but firm. He had beautifully sculpted cheeks with a strong jaw and chin. It made him look determined and strong. Adam obviously noticed her perusal because he grinned and stopped talking. He reached up and pushed her partially dry hair off her neck and shoulder. He let his arm run down her back slowly and linger at the base. Adam set the tray and their glasses aside and moved closer to her on the bed. For a second she felt the panic come back. She should be afraid, and she was, but she was as equally fascinated. Nora felt a primal attraction to him that might have been deniable under different circumstances but not now. The fear and insecurities she recently experienced made her crave the protection of this strong and powerful man. This was a man who held people's lives in his hands, for better or worse. He was also companionship where no other was available. Her thoughts lightly skipped over this path as she touched his face shyly. Her hand moved to his shoulder as he leaned into her. There was nothing shy about the way he captured her mouth in a kiss. It only lasted a minute, but it felt like he was pouring liquid passion from his body into her own. He touched her back and stroked her hair but hesitated before moving to more intimate areas. He was waiting for her to give him a sign that it would be acceptable. She was afraid to cross that line because once she did there would be no turning back. It was not like being a teenager experimenting then quickly saying no before it was too late. This was a man who was used to getting whatever he wanted. Nora knew this should make her angry since she was obviously following his plan but it didn't. She was tired of being scared and wanted to be cast adrift from the nightmare she'd been living. She was sick of fear. She leaned closer to him and reached her hand under his arm around to his back so she could be closer to him and rub her hand down his back. She turned her face up to look at his. He looked down at her and slowly leaned forward until their lips met again. They were warm and dry and just as soft and firm as they had looked. He tasted like wine. It started more gently than the previous passion assault but soon she responded more enthusiastically, which he returned. They began to feed off each other's hunger with kisses and touch. The line had been crossed and she didn't question her decision. Her skin was tingling and sensitive. Every sensation was like electricity zipping through her body. Nora's skin was on fire with desire for him. The sense of urgency was overpowering. Their breathing became deeper and faster. His hands brushed across her nipples under her shirt and her need intensified. She felt herself getting desperate for what was building but also frustrated with the agonizing slowness. She unbuttoned his shirt and ran her hands across his chest, taking in his heat and the smell of his warm, aroused body. He smelled good and clean and had a unique smell that men have. It was intoxicating. She pushed his shirt over his shoulders and it was off in a second. He pulled her shirt over her head. The air was cool enough to cause her to shiver. He noticed immediately. He draped his shirt over her shoulders as he stood up. It was still warm from his body and smelled deliciously like him.

"I'll be right back. Don't move," he said quickly, with an intense look on his face. She had no intention of going anywhere. Nora wanted him as much as she knew he wanted her. True to his word Adam walked back into the room less than three minutes later. He was carrying a comforter and two pillows. She placed the pillows as he spread out the comforter on the bed. They stood beside the bed as he pushed his shirt off her and on to the floor. She slipped off the shorts as he took off his jeans. He held the edge of the comforter up as they quickly climbed into bed and under the cover. The combined heat of their bodies made them warm very quickly. Nora ran her hands over his smooth warm skin and enjoyed his strong hands moving expertly over her body. He nibbled her ear lobes, firmly. It wasn't painful, but just not. It reminded her of the near conflict with the towel. Adam must have picked up on the change because he stopped what he was doing. He was propped up on his elbow, looking down at her face. His other hand was still proprietarily placed on her breast, though not moving.

"What is it?" He asked. His look was so intense. She could feel his erection pressed against her hip, which was somewhat of a distraction. How could she tell him what she was thinking when she didn't really know herself?

"Do you want to stop?" He asked.

"No," she said.

"Does it feel good?" He asked.

"Oh, very," she breathed. He had started moving his hand on her breast as soon as she said she didn't want him to stop. Gathering her thoughts had been difficult before. It was impossible now as he rolled her nipple between his fingers.

"What do you want me to do?" He said. She looked in his eyes and saw them dark with passion and lust. He looked smug and slightly amused with his power over her. She wanted to be irritated with him, but her need was already too great. He could see it. Even her fear of him only heightened her arousal. He had her, and knew it. She tried to break through it, angered by his arrogance. He pinched her nipple and twisted, hard. She moaned out loud, then closed her eyes, not wanting to see anything else that would distract her from this pleasure. She heard him laugh and didn't care.

"Nora, you didn't answer me. What do you want me to do?" He asked.

"You know want I want," she answered, breathless. He moved his mouth down her body. He sucked one nipple while rolling and pulling the other. She couldn't keep her body still. Waves of pleasure were building until she didn't think it would be possible to continue.

"Say it, Nora," he said. How could she speak? He continued down across her stomach with his mouth, the scratch from his chin sending chills up her spine. He rested his chin on the mound between her legs and looked up at her. His hand left her breast and he was still. She looked down at him.

"Nora," he said.

"Yes," she answered, still breathless from everything he'd done.

"Do you want me to fuck you with my mouth?" He asked. Oh my.

"Yes," she answered.

"Then say it," he said. She knew her face had been flushed with desire before, but now it burned with embarrassment. She paused a second, then said it because she really wanted him to do it.

"Please, fuck me with your mouth," she said. His eyes met hers in acknowledgement of his small victory. Her eyes flashed angry for a second before his mouth covered her. He licked gently to start, and then gradually increased pressure. There were no more thoughts, only passion burning, and building. It couldn't last much longer. She wouldn't last much longer. She moaned out loud as he sucked, hard. Then he slipped his finger inside her at the same time as he pinched her nipple. She screamed as the orgasm racked her body with spasms. Wave after wave of pleasure crashed through her. Adam continued to suck and draw out each one, until all that was left were shuddering aftershocks. Her body tingled all over as he crawled up and found her lips. His lips were swollen, wet, and warm. He kissed her deeply, making the tingling more intense. He stopped the kiss and reached for his jeans on the floor. His other hand was still on her breast. She had a second of nervousness, wondering what he was reaching for on the floor. Would he hurt her after all? His hand on her breast didn't hurt, but it was firmly, possessively there. Nora didn't try to move, just watched him as he sat back up. Adam looked down at her with his hair messed up, swollen lips and dark eyes. He wanted her. Even if his very hard erection hadn't been lying on her stomach, she would have known how much he wanted to have sex right now.

"What do you want now?" He asked.

"I want you," she said. He smiled beautifully and lowered himself down to kiss her again. His hand reached down to touch the place his mouth had recently given so much attention. He moved his kiss to her nipple and sucked there, just hard enough. It was as if the places were connected by a wire that began to sizzle with electricity. After giving the other breast the same attention he moved back to her mouth. His finger moved in and out, slowly. She was dying to have more in there. She needed to be filled and began to ache with that need. After a lingering kiss he said "Yes, but what do you want me to do? You have to say it, Nora." Really? Not this again. Well, if this was what it took to bring an end to the exquisite pain.

"I want you to fuck me. Now, please," she asked. He handed her a condom, which must have been what he was getting out of his jeans. As she opened the packet he straddled her, and moved up her body so she could reach him. He was quite large, hovering above her stomach. She circled her hand around his penis and squeezed, gently. He was so hard but his skin was so smooth. She ran her hand up the length until her thumb caught the edge of the head, and then rubbed all the way around it. Adam's breathing caught. She stroked her hand down the length until she found his scrotum underneath. She gently held them in her hand and moved them around, using a little pressure, but not too much. Adam was breathing harder now. She realized it might not just be arousal. It must take a certain amount of trust to let someone squeeze your balls, even if you are on top. She looked up at him. He was staring at her, mostly with lust but maybe a little something else she hadn't seen before too. He bent forward some to squeeze her breast. Now she was gasping again. If she didn't get the condom on soon she wouldn't be able to make her hands work well enough to do it. He watched her put it on. She stroked her hand up and down one more time before she released him. Adam gave her a quick smile then lifted himself off of her. As soon as the pressure of his weight was no longer on her legs they spread open for him. He settled right back in like he'd never left. He leaned over, kissed her, and nuzzled her neck. She was breathing rapidly and noticed that Adam was too. He looked at her with barely controlled passion. He whispered in her ear, "Are you sure you want this Nora?"

"Yes, I want this," she said.

"You don't have to if you don't want to," he whispered, softly. What a strange thing to say. He had played her body like a maestro and she was close to having another orgasm. She knew she could have said no earlier, but it was too late now. If he left her alone with this need, it would be torture.

"I know. I want you so much. Please, don't leave me like this," she said. Nora hated to plead, but there was something in his voice that told her he was considering not going through with it. She wrapped one of her legs around his hip. She wanted him so urgently that she would have continued to convince him but Adam rolled over her and his face hovered above. He gently lowered his lips and kissed her. Then he entered her slowly but forcefully. When he was fully sheathed she gasped with the pleasure of such fullness. Each stroke was an unbelievable increase in pleasure from the last. She wanted it to go on forever but knew it would only be a matter of seconds until she would be unable to stop the explosion. It came over her like a sudden violent storm. Nora called out but was unaware as it was all part of such a torrent of passion that she couldn't be sure of anything except the blinding pleasure she had just experienced. As the few last remaining waves of bliss washed through her, she began to be aware of her surroundings. Adam had finished as she did. Nora opened her eyes and looked at him, realizing that he had been watching her. She felt a little embarrassed by this, but his expression was tender, not mocking so she relaxed again. Adam rolled over to her side and held her tight. She felt so comfortable and relaxed at that moment that all she wanted to do was fall asleep. She didn't though, because she was afraid she would wake up alone. She didn't want to be alone because she was afraid to face all the thoughts and doubts she had suppressed that day. She rolled toward Adam. His eyes were closed but she knew he wasn't asleep. He felt her looking at him and opened his eyes.

He smiled and said, "You were incredible. I can't believe how intense that was. Don't tell me you're ready to go again?"

"No, I'm absolutely satisfied," she answered. Nora wanted to ask what came next but she was afraid to hear the answer.

"Are you hungry, do you want a snack?" He asked.

"No, but I could use some more water," she answered. "I also need to go to the bathroom." It was a reminder of the other Adam. The Adam who had taken her and killed Allen. It was not the same Adam in bed with her now. She had separated the two.

"Sure, let's do that first and you can get cleaned up. Then I guess we need to discuss what happens after that," he said. She tried not to guess what he was going to say because she didn't want to be disappointed. Frankly, she didn't know what she would want him to say. There was no future with him. At some point the shock would wear off and there would no longer be two Adam's, just the one and everything he'd done. And what kind of life did he lead? Could a professional assassin be a family man? No, of course not. All she could hope for was to be released, and that would be a miracle. Or she could hope to stay alive long enough for her parents to make someone find her. She knew her father had connections with politicians through his business and contacts with the FBI. Surely he could convince someone to look for her, not that she had any hope they would be able to find her. Adam was no dummy and neither were the other guys with him. They slowly got out of bed and Adam handed her his shirt since it went to her knees. He put on his jeans and pulled out the blindfold, which she stepped into without comment. Adam busied himself starting the shower while she relieved herself. She felt better since he had not reverted to the old Adam. She jumped in the shower and washed her body quickly, but not her hair again. Adam stepped in and washed himself. It was not at all alarming but felt quite natural that he did. They dried off, she brushed her teeth again, not knowing when she would get another chance, and was escorted back to her room. As soon as he took off the blindfold she asked him if he would stay with her. He was very serious and looked into her eyes before answering. He could tell how much she didn't want to be left alone.

"I would love to stay the night with you but I have some things that I have to do. I will get them done and come back as soon as I can. It may be late so don't wait up but I promise I will only sleep in this bed tonight," he said. She was disappointed but felt it was a reasonable compromise. He probably had to report what he found out from her, although what it could possibly be was a complete mystery.

Adam was probably right; she was better off not knowing. But on the other hand how could she protect herself if she wasn't working with any of the facts. She didn't understand anything that was going on but many other people seemed to know more than she did. And evidently she was part of it although Nora couldn't imagine how she was a significant player. She made the decision that she needed all the information, no matter how dangerous. How much more trouble could she be in? She tried to console herself with the thought that she didn't so much want Adam as she wanted the company and security of his presence, no matter how temporary it might be. It bothered her that she wasn't mourning more for Allen. Maybe it was shock or just self-preservation but it wasn't as devastating as it should have been to lose the man she had been dating. In retrospect they spent very little time together. He traveled frequently and she worked quite a bit. They had only dated for a few months but he had really swept her away. He was so committed and serious, but fun. He didn't seem to ever have any doubts they were a great match. And they did always have a great time. He never had bad days or days when he wasn't interested in getting together, except when he was out of town obviously. It sometimes made her feel uncomfortable because she did have bad days and times when she wanted to do things with her friends or her family. All her friends said he was too good to be true, but it didn't seem healthy to be suspicious just because he was a nice guy. She never had any reason to doubt anything he said. But if she was so confident Allen was Mr. Wonderful then why didn't she ever let her parents meet him? They had asked several times for her to bring him to a dinner or get-together but she always had an excuse. Not only was she not completely sure about him but he didn't show any interest in meeting them. He asked a lot about them and the business but was unavailable the few times she tried to set up a casual meeting. It never bothered her that it didn't work out. She was relieved. Instead of looking for a reason to justify her cold response to his probable death she should be considering what was wrong with her. Allen had done nothing to deserve what happened to him. He was an innocent victim brought into all this because of his concern for her. Her thoughts drifted from one thing to another but she finally fell asleep.

She woke from a deep sleep to the sound of the door opening. She was aware of someone coming into the room quietly but did not open her eyes or move. She was so sleepy the effort seemed too great. Nora was in a dreamy state and expected to feel Adam crawl into bed and snuggle up to her. She was completely unprepared for the hand that clamped down over her mouth. She opened her eyes but couldn't see anything since the lights were still out. She used both arms to try to pull his away but he didn't budge, instead using his other arm to grab both of hers, pinning them above her head. He put his face closer to her. She smelled cigar and bourbon.

"If you make a single sound I will kill you. I'm tempted to break your jaw right now to show you I'm not bluffing. But I can think of better uses for it. Don't give me a reason to change my mind," he said. She didn't recognize his voice but there was no mistaking the sincerity.

"If you understand, nod yes," he said. Nora nodded very slowly, but her mind was racing with what to do. She would not scream unless she had no other option or just couldn't help it. He slowly released her mouth but not her arms. He was straddling her waist but was on top of the comforter. She was glad for the lack of skin contact but was trapped in a cocoon. She could make out his silhouette and the basic shape of his face because of the small amount of moonlight coming through the skylight. What little she saw looked mean and scary but could have been an impression as much as anything else. He seemed to be waiting for her to speak or scream. And she had the feeling screaming was what he wanted. It was almost a dare. It took every bit of control she had not to, but she remained silent. Nora would not give this monster the excuse he wanted. After what seemed like an eternity he finally spoke.

"You have your father's control, but your innocence must have come from your mother." He said this very softly, but with barely concealed contempt. What was he talking about? How did he know anything about her family? And why would he care? None of this had any connection with her family. She witnessed a random act of violence and had been hunted because someone thought she knew who did it. Maybe they thought she was someone else. She wanted to ask but was afraid since speaking had been forbidden.

"I heard the report Adam gave. This puts you in a difficult spot. Your father should have been more careful than to let his daughter become a pawn in his own game. He considered his family to be untouchable because of his power and influence. He miscalculated terribly. I would have loved to see the look on his face when he found out. I'm sure he's exercising his 'influence' to try and gain control and get you back. What he'll find is he has no influence over us. I doubt he even knows what we truly are. It has been decided that you stay alive and here for now. That was not my decision, but you can guess how I feel about Anderson's. Maybe you have other attributes from your mother that would increase your value. Adam seems to think so. You aren't the hellcat your sister is. I'm glad she wasn't as docile and obedient as you. I think I can break her," the man said. Her heart was racing and mind was spinning. This was not a case of mistaken identity! What did he mean about her sister? They couldn't have her too. She had gone away, unless she came back? She wouldn't believe it. And the sexual innuendo about her mother was sickening. Her father was not some evil man people hated. She felt like she had been thrust into the horrors of Wonderland, which Alice found was not so wonderful either. Thankfully the man began to shift his weight off of her as if he were leaving. She took an involuntary deep breath of relief a second before he leaned forward in her face again.

His lips were not an inch from her cheek when he whispered, his hot breath making her shake with fear, "Do not say a word of this to Adam. You will pay dearly, and if his loyalties are misplaced, he will too. So you could be responsible for both of your deaths or find out that he just used you for the nice piece of ass you are. I promise I wouldn't let that go untried before killing you. It would be a tragedy I couldn't let happen." She didn't see his face because she had closed her eyes when he came so close, but she was sure he was smiling. After what seemed like several minutes of his just breathing and her holding her breath he pushed away, got up and left. What could she have been thinking? Nora had begun to believe everything would be okay and that Adam would take care of her. With this guy in the picture, and who knows how many others, Adam may not be able to save her, even if he was sincere. If she read between the lines she could see Adam had tried to warn her of this. He never said things would be great and she had nothing to fear. He had tried to protect her from the things she knew, but still didn't know. Sleep would not return tonight. As much as she tried to clear her mind it still swirled with conflict and doubt. One thing she did decide was not to mention the visit to Adam. As much as she hated to admit it, the man's reasoning made sense to her and she wasn't willing to test it. She could see no clear benefit and several blatant drawbacks. She stayed in the sleepy limbo of her mind too awake, but her body too tired to move until just after dawn when sleep finally took over in the deceiving safety of daylight.

twelve

"Mr. Anderson, you have a call. Do you want to take it or should I take a message," asked Lulu, the Anderson's maid of 35 years.

"I'll take it Lulu," said Sam Anderson, making his way into the library.

The voice on the phone was hesitant. Jeremy Knight tried to never give his boss bad news. During his years of employment he'd mostly succeeded. Today he had to deliver the worst.

"Mr. Anderson, sir, we don't know where Miss Nora is, or who has her. It looks like it was an elite removal team, but that doesn't make any sense," Jeremy said.

"Well, thank you for that assessment. Now I know why I pay you the big bucks. My daughter is missing. You were supposed to keep her safe, even forcing her to come here, if necessary. She's a nurse, damn it, and you couldn't tail her? Un-fucking-believable," shouted Sam.

"Sam, is everything alright? Are you working? Nora is missing and you're working?" Asked Mrs. Anderson.

"No dear, I'm just giving some instructions for Jeremy to give to the private investigator," answered Sam carefully. The last thing he needed was his wife heaping more guilt on him. In truth, he was not wasting his time with a private investigator since he already had a highly trained, highly paid security team. Jeremy Knight was the chief security officer for his corporation and business holdings and should have been able to handle keeping his daughter safe after witnessing a gang fight. This was not rocket science and she was a nurse, not a spook, so what was the problem? Sam took two deep breaths and began again with Jeremy, being careful to keep his voice low.

"Jeremy, let's agree to revisit how you lost her later and concentrate on finding out who has her and where. Do the police have any ideas?" Asked Sam, with as much patience as he could muster.

"Sir, I was able to get some information from the police. There were a couple of odd things that happened within the last few days and Nora seems to be the common denominator. After the gang bangers there was a peeper at the house where she spent the night, then she was chased through the Peabody and then someone broke into her house and killed one of her neighbors as she was pursued, but she left unscathed after each of these events. The last one is the one of greatest concern. There was a disturbance at the apartment complex where Allen lives and a woman matching Nora's description was led away by four men. She was blindfolded. They were Special Forces types, carrying automatic weapons, according to the witnesses. They got into a Suburban and took off before the cops could get there. I don't think the police have put it all together yet, but Lt. Larry Whitman has taken it on and will probably put the pieces together soon. Sir, I don't see how this could be anything but a coincidence. Miss Nora doesn't have anything to do with the business or anything else. We could stop common street thugs but the description of her abductors doesn't fit that profile at all. Sir?" Jeremy stopped speaking because he wasn't sure if Mr. Anderson was still on the phone, and hoped that he wasn't.

"I'm still here. So what I am to deduct from your report is you think a team of professionals has abducted Nora and it has nothing to do with the fact that she witnessed a murder? Jeremy, I'm not buying it. There is no such thing as coincidence. And even if there were we can't afford to believe in it. Nora may not know anything about the business but someone knows about Nora. I expect we will get some kind of demand or ransom request. She is very valuable to me and I'm sure that's no secret," said Sam.

"No sir" was all Jeremy could say. Mr. Anderson loved his family and that was nothing for which to be ashamed. He had every reason to be proud of them. The problem was that although they were all women, not one of them was without balls. Mrs. Anderson was a pistol and the girls had gotten a double dose of stubborn, bravery and independence, which was a very dangerous combination. It was made worse by the fact their father had many enemies, and they had no idea. The people who knew to be afraid of Sam Anderson were the ones who needed to be. The girls knew nothing, but no one was sure how much Mrs. Anderson was informed. Not my problem, thought Jeremy, but he needed to focus on what was his problem. Jeremy needed to come up with a sound plan and fast because a man in his position, with his boss, didn't just get fired. He knew too much about too many to get to walk away.

"Mr. Anderson, I have a communication bridge set up within the MPD and will use anything they get to help us. They are clueless so far. Also, I'm using some of my other connections to find out if the FBI has any role in this. I doubt it very much, but I'm covering the bases. The team is interviewing all of Nora's known contacts to see if she's just in hiding. Allen hasn't been seen or heard from since the attack. He was not taken with Nora so we can assume he was probably collateral damage," explained Jeremy.

"Fine, thank you Jeremy. Please do everything you can to find her and bring her back safely. Also, make sure that the rest of my family is safe and stays safe. Do whatever is necessary," said Sam, sounding defeated and tired. After he hung up the phone he closed his eyes and rested for a minute before rejoining his wife.

She understood why they couldn't call the FBI but wasn't feeling very understanding at the moment. Laura Anderson was no fool and knew plenty. She just wasn't foolish enough to let people know. Sam was aware, of course, but they had made a deal to never discuss it, ever. If he never told her anything then no one could prove that she knew. Laura just kept her ears and eyes open to protect her girls. Not that it had done much good. There was nothing going on that should have caused this. Laura had her quirks but mostly she was just a tough, smart southern woman in a genteel wrapping. Her father had been a judge so she learned many hard lessons at an early age. Besides the strict household there were many death threats that prompted vacations to the beach for she, her mother, sister, and aunts. They had a great time missing school and playing on the beach but there was always the undercurrent of fear her mother and aunts felt. They were afraid for Daddy. And mother was equally afraid for them. It was no wonder she felt she had to be hyper vigilant with her girls. Not that she had been able to keep Nora safe. For all the guilt she was giving to Sam, the guilt she felt herself was compounded. She should have known. It was ironic that she married a man who lived above the law when Laura had been brought up to have complete faith in the law and justice system. Or maybe not so ironic since it was the great justice system that had been responsible for her father's death. Maybe she felt safer with Sam. He wasn't held to the same rules as everyone else and was therefore not as vulnerable. What Laura didn't understand then was that Sam's position above the law had made him an even bigger target.

thirteen

Helen left Nora and drove to the nearest gas station to fill up for the long drive to Pickwick Lake. She ran in, bought a diet coke to stay awake and hit the road. She felt like hell. There were more sore places on her than she knew she had body parts. All of the adrenaline had worn off and pain set in. Half an hour later she stopped again and got a snack and some ibuprofen. The store clerk looked at her with pity but resisted the urge to ask what had happened. Helen didn't volunteer any information. The pain would prove to be a blessing because it was at the second stop she noticed a car that had been at the last stop. The car was gray and nothing special but the man inside was wearing a hat and she had noticed it. She recognized it the second time she saw it and made some quick conclusions before getting back in the car and driving away. She drove straight to the closest fire station and pulled up to the big doors, honking. Firemen are not crazy about having their engines blocked in so she was noticed rather quickly. She got out and talked to them for a few minutes before leaving from a driveway behind the station. They wanted to call the police but she convinced them she was only being paranoid. She did have to explain her injuries to them. She sped out of the area and made many loops and turns until she was sure she wasn't being followed, then got back on the highway. The two-hour drive on dark, desolate country highways went by slowly but music helped and she got through it.

The road around Pickwick was heavily flanked by trees, which canopied over the road. There were some clearings where the water could be seen. The lake looked like liquid silver in the moonlight, which made the trees look darker in contrast. It was late and not the busy season, so she didn't see another person during her slow trip down the dark, winding roads. The trees were so large that they formed a black blanket between her and the sky. She had been to Monica and Stephan Ross' house before but it had been awhile and not driving at night. Not confident but not lost she continued to make progress, only ready to be there. She felt relief when she turned onto the driveway and followed it, narrow and winding to the house. Then she realized she would have to get out of the car and into the dark before making it to safety. She knew no one had followed her. It would have been impossible on such lonely roads. She would have seen anyone, and no one had been behind her for the last hour. The wind started picking up and she could make out a few silver crowns on the water as it became rougher. The tree limbs rattled and leaves were strewn about. She decided to get out now, before it began to rain. There weren't many lights on since Monica didn't want to draw attention to the fact they were there. They must have been listening for her because as soon as she knocked the door opened. Monica and Stephan were waiting up for her, with a drink. She noticed the shock on their faces as they saw what she looked like. She could imagine it must be terrible by now. All of the bruises were dark and the swelling still intact. She gratefully accepted the drink while Stephan unloaded her bags from the car. She was more than a little relieved not to be going outside again. Stephan came back in with a huge burst of wind that blew leaves into the house. After locking the door Monica sat down and began talking. They started with asking about the drive but quickly moved on to what they really wanted to know. They had many more questions than she had answers. Soon, after some speculation, they all went to bed. Even with the wind gusting she soon fell into a deep, dreamless sleep.

Beating on the door woke them all. Helen sat up in bed. So much for pretending they weren't there. She heard Stephan snap a round in the chamber as he left his room. Monica dashed into Helen's room and pulled her into the closet. They sat on the floor listening as hard as they could. Stephan carefully looked out the kitchen window where he could get a view of the door without standing in front of it. There were two men standing there being pelted with leaves and rain. One man beat on the door again and looked around impatiently. When he turned his head Stephan could see the logo on his hat. It was from Sam Anderson's company. Stephan decided to let them in since he didn't think they would just go away. There were two cars in the driveway, after all. Sam must have sent them to protect Helen or why would they have come from Memphis? After asking who it was and getting the expected response he unlatched the door. They walked in quickly, looking around, and the second man held up a photo to Stephan and decided he was a friendly. Stephan wanted to know how the man had a picture of him but decided now was not the time to ask. He called to Helen and Monica and told them it was okay to come up. They didn't so the three men went down stairs to get them. It took a minute to convince Monica the two men were not holding her husband hostage and she could come out of hiding. Helen recognized one of the men as her father's employee and was greatly relieved. She climbed out of the closet and put on a robe. Through the glass doors to the deck she could see the storm coming in on the lake and shuddered. The moon was completely obscured so it was very dark, except for the frequent shocks of lightning, but the flying debris and rain were good indicators of what was to come. Monica put her arm around Helen and pushed past the men to the hall and up the stairs to the den. They sat down on the sofa and braced for the news that these men must have brought. Stephan stood behind them protectively. But instead of giving bad news, the men wanted information from her.

fourteen

They wanted to know what Helen knew about Nora. She was confused.

"Why hasn't Nora called Dad? She was supposed to go to Allen's house and then call Dad," Helen said. The two men looked at each other and said nothing. The man on the left shifted his weight and reflexively touched the gun in the holster on his hip. He felt guilty about giving her bad news when she had obviously been through a lot herself. When Sam saw his daughter with her face bruised and swollen he would explode.

"Tell me what is going on. Now," she insisted, in her most Laura Anderson voice. Monica and Stephan sat quietly, listening to every word as the two men told them what had happened as best as they had been able to figure out. Helen was able to add a few details they didn't know about. Nora had told her some. Nora told her just enough to make her afraid so she would leave and save herself, but not enough that Helen would stay. Typical of Nora, she thought. She made the decision not to do the same and told them about her close call too. Not that she could have denied it. Her face was like a billboard announcing what had happened to her. As soon as she answered all of their questions the first man made a call on his satellite phone and left the room. Monica and Stephan looked terrified.

"Hey, it's going to be okay now. Dad will get everything figured out and fixed. His security team will find Nora and probably kill whoever did this, right?" She asked the second man. He smiled and nodded.

"Will you be staying here?" Asked Stephan.

"Do you want us to?" He asked Helen, smiling still.

She smiled back and said, "Yes, absolutely!"

"Whether we stay here or not is up to Jeremy Knight and Mr. Anderson but we won't be leaving you no matter where we go," he answered seriously. Helen could tell her friends were beginning to relax some. Rumbling that soon progressed to more bright lightning and booming thunder joined the wind. She could see more trees sway through the window. The ceiling fan on the screened in porch was turning by itself. The lake now had waves. Helen wasn't sure this was the best place to be in a bad storm. By the way the others were looking around, they didn't think so either. If there were to be a tornado it wouldn't take much to knock them off the bluff into the lake. As it was, the dock and boathouse were lunging like a cat on a leash. Maybe ten minutes passed before the first man came back into the room. He was off the phone and looking serious.

"You did the best thing coming here and staying together. In the morning we're going someplace else. This place would be too hard to secure and we'd need more men. We should leave tonight, but right now the storm isn't any safer," he said.

"What are you talking about? We are out of Memphis and who would get us with the two of you here?" Helen asked.

"I don't know exactly what is going on but there is reason to believe this is more than gang related. It's possible the men who have Nora and who tried to get you are highly trained mercenaries. If this were the case we wouldn't be enough. Your father isn't convinced of this but isn't willing to take the chance, and I agree," he answered. Helen felt cold at the thought of Nora being held by soldiers, in who knew what kind of war. She thought about how close she had come to being caught too. She had no doubt about the intentions of the man who tried to get her. If this was some kidnapping for ransom then Nora was safe because she knew dad would give every cent he had to get one of them back. But what if the man who attacked her had Nora? Helen wouldn't think about Nora being at his mercy. She couldn't imagine what her parents must be going through right now. She was so glad she was with friends. She would hate to be alone right now.

fifteen

Nora was happy to be alone. Maybe she would be able to think, figure out what to do. She had to get Adam to take her away from here. She had to get as far from the other man as possible. Then she would tell Adam about what he said. Earlier she had decided not to tell him but was wavering. The more she thought about it she didn't have anything to lose. If she stayed here she would be dead. But she couldn't risk telling Adam here. Nora was sure that she was being watched and had to assume she could be heard too. Adam may have been in on all of it, but she had to at least try.

It was mid-morning and she still hadn't seen Adam. She forbid herself from thinking about the possibility of his being dead too. If that evil man killed him then she had little hope of seeing her family again. She would be killed after being raped. Tears formed in her eyes but she refused to let them fall. She began pacing around the room like a caged animal. Nora decided to stay alert and ready for any opportunity. She felt more determined and less victimized as she got her heart rate up and hoped that adrenaline would make her strong enough. She continued to pace and psyche herself up until the door opened. Adam found her walking around the room with a fierce look on her face. His expression was stunned and confused. This was not the woman he had left last night.

"What's wrong Nora?" He asked.

"What do you mean?" She asked, in a deceptively calm voice.

"You seem really agitated. I wanted to come back last night but I had to leave to do something. I just got back and came straight here. Nora, please calm down," he asked. She had begun to pace again. His explanation sounded okay but it didn't make her feel any better. He couldn't protect her if he wasn't here and he would have to leave again. She began to hit the wall as she walked by. Not hard, but rhythmically. Adam began to look worried.

"This isn't because I didn't come back last night is it?" He asked. She exploded at the absurdity of it.

"What do you think? I have been stuck here for days, drugged, fed sporadically and threatened. So you think I'm upset because you didn't

106

sleep in my cell with me last night? I will not be a victim anymore. If I'm to be abused, hurt and killed it will include me fighting with every bit of strength I have," she growled. She did her best to control her rage because she didn't want to shout. He might hear her. And she was afraid of him.

"I didn't think what we had last night was abuse. I did what I had to do but have tried to make it as okay as I could, within my power," he said solemnly. She stopped walking, turned, and snapped back.

"That's just it. You aren't in power so you can't protect me." She hadn't meant to say that, but she was so angry. She was angry with him, her father, that awful man, and with herself for feeling guilty about hurting Adam.

"What are you talking about?" He asked. Nora didn't answer. She looked at him for a moment and then turned away. She may not have uttered a word but her eyes said enough. She was afraid. No, she was panicked but it didn't make sense. She had been fine when he left her.

"I don't want to talk about it," she said. She couldn't tell him but she wanted to give this stress to him. She was about to have a full panic attack. He started to walk toward her and she jumped backed toward the wall. He stopped and she stopped. They were getting nowhere and he knew it. He walked to the opposite wall and sat down on the floor. She sat down on the floor on the opposite side of the room.

"Are you ready to talk about this?" He asked.

"I can't," she answered. She wouldn't look at him, just at the floor.

"You can't or you won't?" He asked.

She looked him in the eye and said, "I can't. Not here."

"Where? What are you talking about? Nora, I don't understand. Tell me what happened while I was gone," he said. Adam was trying to think of what could have happened last night. If she didn't calm down he would have to sedate her. He couldn't take the chance of the rest of the team finding out that he had lost his control over her. If his men knew she wasn't under his influence someone else would want to take over and the methods would be quite different from Adam's. She was beginning to sound more relaxed. Really it was closer to surrender.

"Adam, I would like nothing better to tell you what I am feeling right now, and would if I felt I was in a safe place. You can't change what has happened but you can save me from more of it. Please, take me away from here. I'm not asking you to let me go, just take me

107

someplace under your control," she pleaded.

"Nora, you don't understand what is going on here. I am the buffer between you and some pretty scary guys. I can't just take you away when I want to. I will do what I can to help but you have to tell me what the hell is going on," he answered. "Please," he thought. "Please tell me so I can fix this. She has no idea what is at stake here." Nora got up and walked over to Adam and sat beside him on the floor.

"Adam, I'm sorry. Maybe I'm just going crazy. This is hard and I guess I'm not as tough as I thought," she said, leaning on his shoulder. Adam was confused by this sudden change of attitude but was happy that it at least appeared he had regained power. He hoped it was enough. He reached out and put his arm around her. She moved in closer, letting him know it was okay to touch. Her face looked calm enough, but she was still breathing quickly, like she was still panicked. He didn't want to shatter the peace so he said nothing but continued to move closer to her as long as she was sending the welcome signals. After several minutes of tentative touching he kissed her gently. She kissed him back then moved to kiss his neck, and then ear. As she lightly licked the outside of his ear she began to whisper. Adam went from sucking in his breath at her touch to a different kind of concentration as she told him every detail of what happened during the night. She would stop every few words and suck his earlobe or change to the other ear. Her hands never stopped caressing his chest and shoulders. He closed his eyes to concentrate on what she was saying as he was very distracted by what she was doing. Because of this it took a few minutes for what she was saying to sink in to his aroused mind. He began to get angry and started to pull away from her but she wrapped her arms around him tighter and shifted over into his lap. He became so alert she was afraid he would not be very convincing. She moved until she was straddling his legs, facing him.

She put her hands in his hair and pulled his face into hers and very quietly asked him, "Are they watching or listening, or both?" She continued the erotic charade as she waited for his response. She knew he was having difficulty controlling his strong male urges to fight or to have sex.

"Watching," he finally answered as he put his hand on her breast. She couldn't do this. She couldn't continue doing this now that she knew they were watching. Nora thought they were probably monitoring the room but now that she knew they had an audience she felt sick. Had they been watching last night? Of course they had. Did they watch her in the shower? Adam could feel her pulling away, mentally and physically.

"No baby, we can't stop now. Trust me. It's important and it has to look real and natural. Let's just take it slowly so I can think and we can talk without causing suspicion," he said. "Please," he thought. "Get control and trust me." She knew what he was saying made sense so she tried. She just couldn't do it like this so she pushed away from him and stood up. He looked afraid now. She smiled at him and offered him her hand. He took it and stood up. She led him to the bed. He took off his shirt and pants and climbed in. She took off her shorts as she slipped into bed and feigned a shiver so he snuggled her up under the covers to stay warm. Now they could talk and do everything else without as much scrutiny. During this whispered, broken conversation he let her know how important it was for them to appear normal and she appear docile and obedient. She let him know she expected him to do something to save her and to tell her what was going on. During this conversation the foreplay couldn't, and didn't stop. It had to look like rising passion and they were going to have to finish the show, convincingly. He assured her more time to talk after but told her to stop now and get into the sex. She was stiff and hesitant. Adam began to concentrate his efforts on her arousal. He knew that if he could get her far enough along she wouldn't care who saw what. She stopped fighting it and let him take over, starting with removing her shirt. He used her fear and anger and turned it into passion. The covers let her pretend they were alone. His lips caught hers. No longer whispering in between kisses, his tongue could sweep through her mouth and capture hers. Adam squeezed her breast, gently but firmly. His mouth made its way to her nipple, leaving a trail of soft kisses down her neck. He rolled one nipple while sucking on the other. With each touch, and taste, she cared less about anything going on except what they were doing. Nora's breathing was faster and her legs shifted under the covers. Adam started to move down her body. Nora grabbed his head to stop him.

"No," she whispered.

"What? You loved it last night," he answered, softly. Nora's face burned.

"Yes, I did. But I didn't know I had an audience. Now I do. I won't be able to forget," she said, softly. As she spoke, she pulled him up to her again. Adam lay down beside her. She kissed him briefly, and then started working her way down his body, while remaining under the covers.

"What are you doing, Nora?" He asked, surprised.

"I assume you don't mind being watched," she said.

"No, I don't mind at all," he said, leaning back on the pillows, arms behind his head. She worked her way down and settled between his legs. The covers were just over her head so she could get fresh air, but no one could really see her. She held him in her hand to feel how hard he was. As she touched him with her fingertip, she blew softly. She circled the head with the tip of her warm tongue before putting her mouth over him completely. As she took him in her mouth each time she circled him with her tongue. Every few strokes she would take him very deep, into her throat, and pause for a few seconds before starting again. Adam's breathing became deep and erratic. Nora varied the rhythm enough to keep him from finishing too soon. As soon as she tasted the little weep that comes before climax she stopped. Nora crawled up his body and looked at the dazed expression on Adam's face.

"Wow," he said. He grabbed Nora and flipped her onto her stomach. He straddled her legs and covered her body with his. Sweeping her hair over one shoulder, he kissed her ear then tugged on her earlobe with his teeth. His hands burrowed under between her body and the bed. He squeezed both breasts and thrust down with his pelvis, which pushed hers into the bed. The pressure from all those places and his stiff erection across her backside were enough to make her moan, loudly. He continued to slowly thrust, and squeeze, and then gently bit her neck. Nora's body tingled with excitement. Adam brought one of his legs down and wedged it in between hers. He lifted her onto her knees as he brought the other leg around. Nora turned her head around to look at Adam as his hands found her left breast and clitoris. She had to lock her elbows to keep from pitching forward at the onslaught of sensation. Her knees were spread wide to accommodate his large, muscular thighs. She could feel his erection pressed against her, but he didn't push forward. Adam took his hand off her breast and put it on the bed just outside her left arm. He was covering her body. His right hand hadn't moved from where it was gently, lazily making circles. Nora was beyond ready. He seemed to know this and his hand stilled, but didn't leave her. Adam whispered in her ear, his lips so close they touched.

"Nora, do you want me?"

"Yes," she said.

"Are you sure you want to do this? You don't have to," he said.

"I want to. I want you. Please," she said. He kissed her ear and smiled. He put a condom on quickly, then gave her a few more circles to compensate for the distraction of conversation. He knew she was wet and ready for him. Feeling her heat but not entering her had been very difficult, but the payoff was worth it. He filled her in one stroke. She cried out. He paused, afraid he had hurt her. Instead of pulling away, she moved against him so he started moving again, faster. It didn't take long for them to reach their goal and neither gave a thought to spectators. As they lay together under the covers he assured her he would work out what to do but he still couldn't tell her anything. She was hurt by his lack of trust but had no recourse. There wasn't anything for her to do and she as too exhausted to think. She fell asleep in his arms.

He was nowhere near sleep, annoyed at the new problem, which could have so easily been avoided. What Sid did was counterproductive. There was nothing to gain. Sid was only acting on his sadistic urges. And Sid was truly a sadist. Adam didn't doubt a single word of Nora's telling of what happened. Actually she was very lucky to have been unharmed. There was no point in talking to Sid. Nothing happened but promises of violence. It could be argued that it furthered their cause, although Adam didn't believe that to be true. Even men like Sid were a useful part of the team. Adam found him to be a useful employee, if somewhat difficult to control. While he recognized Adam was the leader, he would only follow directions as long as it contributed to his own goals. Adam knew this and allowed for it. Sometimes his special talents were the only things that worked. He hoped that would never be the case with Nora.

sixteen

City Hall was a busy place on any given day. There were clerks and assistants, security, elected officials, and unfortunately sometimes reporters. The Mayor loved to see all of the hustle and bustle, and loved to see his power and influence reflected in the eyes of those around him. He was a man to be respected in the city of Memphis. He felt supremely responsible for the successes of the city. The only reason he couldn't do more was because of the city council. They were shortsighted and didn't have the trust of and respect for his office they should have. He needed money and room to maneuver to get things done. Instead they were always scrutinizing and questioning everything. They treated him with contempt at times, and that couldn't be tolerated. The mayor went to the mirror and straightened his tie and smoothed his suit. He would be on camera today and would look good. This dark suit wasn't his favorite but it was perfect for the funeral he would attend. He checked his handkerchief. It was clean and he would give it to the grieving mother if he got an opportunity. And he would. He had people to take care of things like that. He was working on what he would say to the press after the funeral when one of his aides walked in and stood at the door. The mayor didn't acknowledge him and the man wouldn't speak until spoken to. This was a power play used by the mayor to remind his people who was in charge. The aide would have to wait several minutes for the mayor to make eye contact and speak first. The mayor heard regular reports about what was going on in his city. He had a hand in everything that was anything. The times when he had been shut out he made sure to exact a payment. One thorn in his side had recently been snipped down to nothing. A Memphis family with deep roots in political power had struggled with him for dominance over the city for years. They had a large population of the community behind them in whatever they wanted to do. If his support were because of the people's genuine respect, that would be called democracy. But this influence had more to do with a combination of threats and bribery. The mayor and this family were both well-connected black leaders in a city where there was a black majority. The mayor had used well-placed contributions to community leaders

112

and sending around his security to influence the poor of Memphis, and there was no shortage of poor in Memphis. The other family did the same. Election time was the scariest for these people. Vans would drive around the neighborhood to 'help' people get to the polls. Sometimes money or beer would be given for the ride back home. It was not unheard of for the dead to come back to life to support an influential candidate. The mayor had dealt a hard blow by contributing, indirectly of course, to a federal investigation of this family. When the indictments came down it was cause for celebration in his office. With this family out of power he would be the undisputed ruler. There were some white men of influence but they would never get far in Memphis politics. There were too many black voters and the pain of white oppression was permanently imprinted on them. They would rather have a corrupt black leader than an honest white one (assuming an honest politician of any race could be found). He fit the bill.

As he was driven to the funeral he went over the case in his mind so he would look every bit the mourner. This was a kid who was academically strong and a sports star at his high school. He was popular among students, teachers, and his community. Dedrick was a kid for whom everyone would grieve. And that was exactly what the mayor needed.

seventeen

Sam Anderson sat at his desk and stared at his phone. He wasn't really looking at it, just fixing his eyes on it while listening to Jeremy give the latest report. He didn't like what he was hearing. Jeremy was giving a synopsis of what happened to Helen. It made him feel physically sick to think of someone hurting his daughters. It was beyond belief. Who had targeted his family? He could think of people who would have reason to but no one who would dare. And who would have the juice to take Nora without a trace? He was the one who could make that happen and he didn't do it. Locals did not execute this. Jeremy would have been on them immediately if it were someone around here. He made it his business to know what was going on. Sam had made some ultimatums lately that were unpopular, including to the mayor, but not to anyone with these resources. Why hadn't they heard from anyone about demands or ransom? None of it made any sense. Nora wouldn't be able to tell them anything so she must be a bargaining point. But no one had tried to bargain. Jeremy had some theories but they were little more than guesses. Sam knew they were no closer to finding Nora and the more time went by the less likely it would be to get her back alive. Jeremy knew that Sam couldn't risk the scrutiny of the FBI therefore he couldn't call them for help. The only chance they had for outside help would be from the Memphis police, but they would go to the feds. It made Sam angry to even consider outside help so Jeremy didn't mention it. Sam didn't think he should have to do that since he paid to maintain an entire security force. Jeremy agreed since it was his job security but he didn't have the resources to handle this. These were not locals and were well trained and organized. Jeremy was used to having the upper hand since his group was made up of highly trained former military. They had been picked out for their expertise and discretion. Usually they only had to flex their muscles, not actually use them. As far as corporate security went they were the best. But they were out of their league with the group that took Nora. Sam finally stopped staring and made eye contact with Jeremy.

"What about this Lt. Whitman? Do you think he can be brought in?"

Asked Sam. Jeremy sighed as he thought about the question. He had already considered this but had rejected the idea because everything he knew about Whitman was above board. That didn't mean he wouldn't but it would be a gamble.

"I don't know Mr. Anderson. He hasn't gone that way before but it can't be ruled out. I could do some trolling," he suggested.

"Do that. And if you think he won't bend that way then work a different angle. Find me some answers. I don't care how you do it," said Sam. Jeremy nodded and left the room. He had been dismissed. Sam continued to think about why anyone would take Nora except for ransom. None had been requested so that wasn't it. This wasn't the first time he had been afraid for Nora's life. When she was eight she had been taken from their home during a party. It had taken two days to get her back but they did. It had taken a hefty price but she was returned, mostly unharmed. To this day Sam didn't know exactly what happened during those two days. Nora hadn't wanted to talk about it and the psychologist had instructed them not to pressure her. After many months of counseling she seemed fine so Sam and Laura didn't want to remind her of the ordeal just to ease their curiosity. They knew some of the basics. The physical exam showed she had not been raped. She had some bruises and welts but nothing too serious. She had been able to give some general descriptions and accounts of what happened but that was it. She never gave them a single name or even how many people were involved. She was never able to tell them where she had been held other than that it was probably a house. It had been difficult for the entire family. The nanny had been putting Helen to bed when Nora sneaked out of her room to watch the party. The police speculated that she went outside and then she was taken. Sam had called the police then and that was the main reason he didn't want them involved now. They did nothing to find her and hampered Sam's response when the kidnapper's demand did come. The kidnappers wanted Laura's father, Judge Hunt, to decide in favor of a criminal who was appealing a conviction. The case was not high profile and the crime hadn't been especially heinous but Judge Hunt was going to find against this man. When Sam went to him with the demand he agreed to do it if Sam promised never to tell Laura or anyone else, no matter what. Sam agreed. The judge overturned the conviction and the man went free. Sam got Nora back, mostly fine. The judge had instructed

Sam to take the family away immediately after Nora's return because he was going to have the man arrested and his judgment changed based on intimidation. Laura's father played hardball and evidently everyone knew it because the next day he was killed. Sam started to build his security team shortly after that. He didn't want to feel that powerless ever again. Yet here he was. This was worse because there were no demands to be met. He had no power or influence over these people. There would always be bigger fish. Maybe it was time to retire. If Nora came back. No, when Nora came back. She had to be okay. If she wasn't, he may as well die too.

eighteen

The mayor's car drove up to the front of a large, beautiful church in the medical district in Memphis. There were many people making their way in or talking in small groups outside the church. Good, he thought. There were the news vans. He straightened his tie and smoothed his hair before getting out of the car. His driver timed walking around the car slowly enough so that the reporters could see he had arrived. Just as he opened the door and the mayor stepped out, the cameras were on him. He wouldn't comment now, but would after the funeral when Mrs. Ray was at his side. He sat a few rows behind the family but close enough to the front that most people would see him. There were hundreds of people seated in the church already, but it was nowhere near full. He casually looked around at the nicely decorated, modern church. There were video screens so every person in the congregation could feel that they had a front row view. There were many teenagers present which wasn't a surprise. Dedrick had been a popular kid. He wished that some other kid had been chosen. He felt some twinges of guilt but reminded himself that the boy's sacrifice would not be wasted. He would make sure that good would come from this. He knew the city of Memphis would benefit from his staying in charge. No one else could take the city where he could. Many more kids would be hurt and killed without his plan for the city. He was going to make Memphis as big as Atlanta, maybe bigger. It was on its way there now and would be further along if not for the city council. He intended to blame them for this child's death. He would remind everyone about the city council's refusal to raise taxes, which was followed by extensive budget cuts. He would make them pay. They thought to control him by tightening the purse strings. He would not let anyone keep him from greatness. He was chosen by God to raise this city up. It would be the new standard and all by him.

The coffin was closed of course. Music was playing softly. There were sounds of crying, even wailing by friends and family. Sad, shocked faces looked around as if they might see something that would explain this horrible thing, or maybe get some relief from it. But they looked in vain because all they saw were the reflections of their pain on the people around them. He was ready for things to get going because he knew it wouldn't be quick. He used the time to collect his thoughts for the press. His face was solemn and composed as his intelligent mind spun through every angle and how best to make his case.

Mary Ray knew this was the worst day of her life. She had been in a fog of grief so oppressive that she knew she would never be free of it. How could she live when one of her babies did not? She knew she had to be strong for the girls but she just couldn't. She was out of strength. There just wasn't any left. Sheila and Tiffany must have known this because after the first night they stopped trying to lean on her. They both had aged years in a few days. They lost their older brother and the mother they knew and counted on. The numbness was still blessedly there and they didn't want to feel. Not anything, ever again. The music played, the preacher preached, people came by Mary's seat and muttered blessings and condolences but none of it penetrated the fog. The three remaining Ray's just nodded and tried to smile and respond but nothing really came out. Mary Ray was a good Christian woman and knew she should find some comfort from all of the blessings, but there was no comfort for her. You couldn't feel comfort if you couldn't feel. And to allow feelings was something she just couldn't do. The pain was too severe. She couldn't breathe with that pain. No, she would just stay in the numbing fog of grief until she died, and she hoped it would be soon. Death would make it all stop. And then she could see Dedrick again. The girls would be better off without her anyway. She couldn't do anything to help them. Now they had to take care of her. She was no longer a whole person and never would be again. When the service was over it was almost a surprise. She wasn't sure she had heard anything said. The hostesses, dressed in white, came and led the three Ray's out behind the coffin. Once they were outside the hostesses led them over to a cluster of reporters and a tall man in a suit. Through the fog they realized it was the mayor and allowed themselves to be shuffled to his side as he spoke. None of them heard a single word he said and didn't care. Mary accepted his handkerchief and reflexively dabbed at her dry eyes. She could cry no more. The Ray's were ready to be home and to be alone. They wanted to escape this misery but each knew it wouldn't be possible.

nineteen

Mr. Anderson watched the evening news and listened closely as the mayor spoke at Dedrick Ray's funeral. His statement was impassioned and made a good case against the city council and a good case for an increase in taxes. The common citizen would be moved, especially after seeing the grief written all over the woman's face and the two young girls looking so innocent and so lost. It caused him pain to see those girls and to think of his own. How did things get so out of hand? He had heard from Jeremy. Helen was safe now and on her way back to town. But Nora was still gone and no one could tell him where. It just didn't make sense. Who would want her? Even if it was to get to him, who cares that much? This was local politics, nothing that big. Jeremy swears they were professionals and he should know. But who? It seemed more military in nature but that was ridiculous. He had nothing to do with anything military or national much less international. This was not the style of any legitimate law enforcement agency. Even the local police couldn't pull this off without a trace. Besides, the mayor had them in his pocket. The FBI and MPD are the only ones who would be interested in anything Sam was involved in. Sam had called some friends and asked some vague questions but Jeremy had been doing the real searching and had found nothing. Sam would turn everything he had over if it would bring back Nora, but he didn't think it would make a difference. He poured a drink and sat in a chair. He turned off the lights and looked out the window. Nothing. He sat like that until he had finished his drink. He missed Laura but was glad she wouldn't be here to see Helen's face. She had finally agreed to leave town after much pressure from he and the girls. He didn't want to see Helen's face. The description was enough. The security guys would be taking her to a safe house and she would not leave until this was over. As much as he wanted to have her here he was afraid that if they came for him she might get hurt again. They had to be punishing him. That was clear after he heard about the attack on Helen. These monsters, whoever they were, were using Nora to hurt him. Sam was beginning to believe it was only that and not as leverage since they hadn't asked for anything. He still had one daughter but would never recover if he didn't have both. He would continue to do everything he could to get Nora back but was starting to be convinced that it would never happen. Now he had to focus on keeping Helen safe, and Laura. It was clear that these people were ruthless enough to take everything he loved. He sent a security team to Laura to keep her safe. She had only been in the hotel for one night. Sam had her change to a beach house, which would be easier to secure. Laura hadn't said a word, which meant she was afraid. Monica and Stephan were going on an extended vacation in Europe, compliments of Sam Anderson with his apologies. They were relieved to get away. Helen would be furious at being kept a virtual prisoner but there was no other way and she had to know that.

twenty

Nora was proving to be a valuable asset. The word on the street was that Sam Anderson would do whatever it took to get her back. Unfortunately for him, that wasn't the goal. She would be kept for a while, just in case, but had probably already given all she had to give. Well, maybe not all she had to give. She would have had a certain amount of value even if she hadn't been Sam Anderson's daughter. Her appeal would cause a problem with a less experienced group, but not this one. This team was picked for unyielding professionalism. It didn't hurt that they were also very well paid. The question was did she have anything else to tell. Adam didn't seem to think so but Sid wasn't sure. He didn't doubt Adam. Sid implied to Nora that he doubted Adam but he didn't really. Adam was damn good at what he did and never made mistakes. His method of control and interrogation was different from Sid's but just as effective. Adam had a way with targets that was impressive to watch. Of course, so did Sid. Even Adam admitted that Sid was a genius at his craft. They used two very different techniques, with very similar results. It really depended on the target. Those impervious to Adam's charm would succumb to Sid's motivation. Sid started to become hard just thinking about Nora being turned over to him. He had planted some seeds of discontent and maybe Adam would lose his hold on her and she would be given to Sid to control. Of course, the client could call at any time and pull the plug on the whole thing. Then there probably would be no Nora. It was all very complicated so there was no way to tell how long they would have her. This job was unusual in that the team hadn't been made aware of the final goals, and only Adam knew the client's identity. Sid didn't like this situation but had to trust Adam. They had worked together for two years. During that time Sid learned to respect Adam's abilities as a team member and a boss. This job was different, but it paid really well. He and Sid were the only members of the group who had English as a first language so the others didn't have direct contact with Nora. They were too good to take a chance in giving any information away. That was one reason they had never been tracked or caught. And that was why they were so expensive. The client could expect to have no trail and therefore no retribution. They weren't perfect but were good at cleaning up any mishaps and they all covered each other. There were no friendships. That could get in the way. They all respected each other's skills and the symbiotic relationship they shared. Members were intelligent enough to know their individual success depended upon the success of the team. Adam had Nora Anderson believing he was a rebel trying to protect her, but he was just manipulating her to make her as compliant as possible. Adam would never risk everything for some pathetic, spoiled bitch. He could have any woman he wanted at any time. He was great at what he did. Of course Sid was no slacker himself. It was easy to be good when you truly enjoyed your work. He could honestly say there was nothing he would rather be doing. Each member of the team brought special skills and talents, all of which were important to the mission. Sid was waiting for a response from Adam. His order to get Nora's sister had been aborted but then an order had gone out to find her, nothing else. Sid truly hoped that he would get a second chance with her. She had been lucky to get away the first time but wouldn't be again. Helen Anderson would be a worthy target. She wouldn't fold so quickly that he wouldn't have time to enjoy it. He knew Nora was too compliant to be really fun. He would take pleasure in dealing with her because she would be afraid and that was part of it, but it wouldn't be the same as with Helen. She would fight and show some real passion. Then she would acknowledge him as her master. Winning wasn't the best part. He always won. The game was what appealed to him. His phone buzzed and he quickly answered it. Yes, he got the order to take her, but not to kill her. Good, he thought with satisfaction. He didn't want her dead. That would be no fun at all.

twenty-one

Helen said goodbye to Monica and Stephan before being taken to the safe house. It was a tearful parting because it had been such a terrible ordeal, which was far from over for Helen. Her friends were happy to be leaving but felt bad about abandoning her. They left with an escort to pack their things and get to the airport. Flying on a chartered jet would hopefully ensure a clean get-away. There was no reason to believe they were of interest at all but Sam wasn't taking any chances and Helen was glad. One of the guards who came to get her from Pickwick was driving the car. They had picked up two more at the rendezvous to drop off her friends. She tried to ask them what the plan was but the only one who would answer was the guard who had been with her longest. She found out his name was Ben. He smiled at her a lot, which made her feel better. The other guards noticed his unusual happiness and began to lighten up a little. They dropped hints about his not being married and told some embarrassing stories. Ben's face darkened by a few shades of red but he didn't get mad. He just laughed at himself. Helen liked that. For the first time in days she wasn't thinking about Nora or being scared. Every time he looked at her in the rearview mirror she felt butterflies in her stomach. She had to concentrate to listen to what he was saying. When she finally focused she realized they were taking her some place other that home. When she asked about it the guards were evasive. She eventually cajoled a straight answer from Ben. She would be going to a safe house and under twenty-four-hour supervision. AKA, house arrest. Helen didn't want to take it out on Ben because she knew he would only be following her father's orders so she called Sam.

"Do you have something to tell me?" She asked.

"Now Helen, you know it's the only solution. You wouldn't be safe anywhere else."

"I won't be much better off than Nora," she said. But even as she said it she wished she could take it back. It wasn't true. Her father was only doing what he thought would keep her safe.

"Sorry Daddy," she said quietly.

"It's okay, Helen. I know this is a nightmare but I couldn't bear it if you were taken from me too. Please do this for me. I can't think of a better way. If you can I'm open to suggestions," he said. She knew he wasn't really open to suggestions but wanted her to think it through, weighing all of the options. Her suggestions would be a way for him to shoot them down, to further convince her he was right. It just wasn't worth it to go down that path. She had done it many times in her life and had never won.

"Okay, I'll do it, for now. But you have to promise to keep me updated. I don't want to feel like a coat put away for the summer," she answered.

"I promise, baby. If you call please use one of the guard's phones. They can't be traced. I love you," Sam said.

"I love you too, Daddy," she answered, with a bit of a pout. It suddenly felt very final. She didn't want to hang up but he already had. She rode in silence for a while, composing herself. After some time she engaged the guards in conversation again to help make things seem less serious. Ben admired her courage and ability to put her worries aside and move on. He watched her as much as he could while still driving safely. She was beautiful, even with a bruised face. The swelling was gone so he could see what she looked like. Even if she hadn't been beautiful he would have been interested in her. She had a quick sense of humor and was passionate about life. Helen also had a streak of stubborn independence that rivaled her father's. Ben had to stop going down this road. She was Sam Anderson's daughter and it would not be okay for him to hit on her. It could mean more than just his job. He tried to keep his mind on the job but couldn't help but listen to her. Her laughter was inviting and he felt it was just for him. Looking around the car he could see that the other guys felt the same way. She had her mother's charm. Ben had met Mrs. Anderson on a few occasions but had never seen Sam's daughters. They had their own lives. He had seen a picture of Miss Nora since they were all trying to find her. She was beautiful too, but she didn't seem to have the fire that Helen did. He was on that dangerous road again. He had to stay off of it.

Helen could tell that he was interested in her. He seemed to respond to everything she said. She could tell he was watching her and she liked it. He was nice looking and had a body hardened by training. For all his tough exterior she could tell that he was a thoughtful and kind person who made her laugh. Why couldn't she have met someone like him socially? Of all the men she had met and the few she had dated, he held the most promise. She had never looked twice at any of her father's employees before. It would be terribly awkward but she couldn't deny the attraction. They pulled into a small parking garage downtown and the door quickly closed behind them. There was only one other car parked. It was a Yukon, just like the one she was in. They were both black with darkly tinted windows and were what the security team drove. They all squeezed into an elevator and got off at what had to be a warehouse that had been converted into condos. This one was beautifully decorated with rich, warm colors and modern but comfortable style. The colors made such a large space still feel inviting. The area was open with the furniture arrangement giving the impression of separate rooms. There were large windows on one side and stairs on the far wall. The upstairs was a loft with a balcony and there appeared to be several rooms with real walls. The kitchen was downstairs and beautiful, with brown granite counters and pristine appliances with a long bar. The open floor plan wouldn't offer much privacy from her guards but the openness would help to make her feel less claustrophobic. She knew no matter how nice the cage, it was still a cage. She hoped Ben would be there often as a welcomed distraction. Ben carried her bags to her room and she followed him up. He set her bags down and turned to leave as she was walking through the door.

"Have you been here before?" She asked.

"Yes, we've had a few people stay here before," he answered.

"I'm sure I don't want to know the circumstances of those visits. Who will be staying with me?" She asked, getting to the point.

"I don't know. That will be up to Mr. Knight. But someone will be here with you the whole time," he said.

"Is it possible that it might be you?" She asked.

"Do you want it to be me?" He asked.

"That would be fun, don't you think?" She replied. He smiled and she smiled back. He didn't know if Jeremy would assign him here but he was going to try to get this assignment. Helen had decided she would just ask Mr. Knight to assign Ben here. It would be difficult for him to tell her no and she would certainly be a better prisoner if she were made happy. She had no doubt that she could convince him to grant her request.

twenty-two

Lt. Whitman had been in a funk for days. Ever since the Ray shooting things just weren't adding up. None of the subsequent events made sense and he couldn't figure out how they were related. He had enough witnesses to be sure that these things really had happened but it was all crazy. And now Miss Anderson's father was making some strange inquiries through his corporate security officer, Jeremy Knight. Mr. Knight had a reputation for being over the top with security and a tough guy. He had even heard some talk of enforcer type intimidation by his team but none of it was substantiated. Why was Mr. Anderson so interested in the investigation now? He had assumed that Nora had gone into hiding or had maybe had a nervous breakdown since she was accusing other detectives of the crime. Now he wasn't so sure. He wanted to find her and talk to her again when she was calm and had rested. There was no answer at her house or her cell phone. There was no answer at her friend or sister's houses. He called Mr. Anderson and was put through immediately.

"Yes, Lt. Whitman. Do you know anything?" Sam asked, a little too quickly. Jeremy had reported not getting very far feeling him out so they assumed he would not be part of the team.

"Mr. Anderson, I would like to ask Nora a few more questions. Could you tell me where I could reach her please?" Lt. Whitman asked.

"I can't really tell you where she is right now," he answered, being deliberately vague. He was trying to decide whether or not to tell Whitman about her disappearance. It would be a calculated risk but he was desperate and Whitman seemed to really be working the case. Whitman could tell that he was hedging and assumed it was because he didn't want anyone to know where she was to protect her.

"Mr. Anderson, if you don't want me to know where she is that's okay. Just have her call me. I don't have to see her," he said.

"It isn't that," Sam said in a resigned voice.

"What is it?" Whitman asked, his curiosity heightened.

"I need to ask for your discretion. If this gets out it will mean my daughter's life. Please assure me that you will not contact the FBI," he said. It was obvious from his voice that he was more pleading than

126

ordering so Whitman relented.

"I'll do the best I can, Mr. Anderson, but you need to tell me what is going on. Where is Nora?" He asked. This was a very strange conversation. Whitman grabbed his pen and the closest piece of paper he could find and took notes as Sam filled him in.

"I don't understand why mercenaries would be interested in your daughter? Or why they would be interested in you," he said. This sounded incredulous. Maybe irrational fears ran in the family.

"I wish I knew. But what other explanation can you give me for the circumstances. Do you really believe that a gang would kidnap Nora and in the way that she was taken. They would just have killed her. Please, give me another explanation," said Sam, getting more distressed by the word.

"I have to admit that the gang theory doesn't seem to make sense given the facts. What happened to Allen Chapman?" Asked Whitman.

"We don't know. No one has heard anything and we can't find him. Really, we are assuming the worst given what the witnesses said," he answered.

"How do you know what the witnesses said?" Asked Whitman.

"Look, what's important now is information sharing and finding Nora. You can't blame me for doing everything I can to find my daughter. I may have asked my staff to overstep their authority but don't fault them. I was desperate," he replied.

"If you were so worried about Nora, why didn't you call the FBI?" Asked Whitman, a little miffed at Anderson's nerve sending in his security team to question the witnesses. He wondered if Sam found out anything they didn't. They probably did, he thought angrily.

"I was afraid to call them. They could have done something to get her killed. You have to understand. The last time they couldn't help her and almost kept me from saving her," said Sam.

"Wait, what do you mean 'last time'?" He asked. Sam took a deep breath and exhaled slowly. He had boxed himself in. He wouldn't be able to spin this. He told Lt. Whitman the story, leaving out Judge Hunt's part in the story. He would only break his promise if it were to save Nora's life. Lt. Whitman let loose an explicative that was very uncharacteristic for him. He could now understand why things didn't add up. He was missing some of the most pertinent facts. It would be a miracle for Nora to come out of this alive. He wasn't able to get much more out of Anderson but knew he could get more information from the reports filed at the time. He gave up on the interview and Anderson agreed to call if he heard anything from the kidnappers but Whitman didn't believe him. After reading the reports and doing a little more research he felt that he at least had an idea what had happened to Nora as a child but couldn't understand how it related to the Ray case. The poor girl had been through more than any child should ever have to. Whitman called the officers who worked the disturbance at Allen Chapman's apartment. After some much needed follow up he found that Allen was also Robert, and Craig. This gave them reason to dig further. Allen did not work for the company the Anderson's thought. Fingerprints taken from the apartment belonged to Craig Burton. Burton had his fingerprints on file from applying for a private investigator's license in Tennessee to work for a company in Nashville. He applied for and received his license five years ago, but never renewed it. What was he doing in Memphis, pretending to be another guy, dating Nora Anderson? Given the new insight he began to look at accusations of the vice detective's involvement with an open mind. After much time and research he began to see a disturbing trend. Some casual conversations with other detectives began to solidify his findings. This was something he couldn't tell anyone until he could prove it without a doubt because he would be accusing some highly decorated and well respected men of serious criminal activity and it wouldn't go well. The three men in question did not only have great authority but were also supported by the mayor. One was even a family member. He was beginning to understand why this case didn't feel right to him.

twenty-three

Nora woke to the sunlight waning. She must have slept for hours and felt like she had a hangover. The stress was finally taking its toll. She wasn't sure how long she could keep this up. She didn't even feel the same comfort with Adam, which wasn't that much anyway. She had come to the conclusion that she wouldn't be able to wait it out or to trust Adam to get her through this safely. The scary man had cast enough doubts that she couldn't take that chance. Of course, coming to the conclusion didn't get her any closer to a solution. And now that she knew she was being watched there were fewer options. Nora wished her father would find her. Playing the martyr was over. Someone had to help her, or she had to escape, no matter what. The only chance would come at night, when Adam was there. So far he had not slept in the room with her but tonight she had to make sure he did. He never locked the door while he was in the room with her. She would be able to open the door and get out. She didn't really think she would make it out of the house, if that was where she was, and to safety but had to try something. Nora couldn't just wait for them to kill her. She was feeling very anxious and wanted to run out now. Success was doubtful because she had the barest of clothes, no shoes, and no idea where they were but still had to try. In order for Adam to sleep through her escape she would have to have some help. Maybe she could entice him with alcohol? How would she get Adam to come tonight, and bring drinks?

Nora was overcome by impotence. She couldn't make or execute even a detail of a plan. She paced around the room and became more panicked. There must be something she hadn't thought about. As she paced she realized she was doing just that. They could see her. So maybe if she seemed agitated someone would tell Adam and he would come in to calm her down. She didn't want to look so crazy they thought she was out of Adam's control but enough so they would get him in there to subdue her. It would be a very difficult role for her. Nora would have to lie and act, neither of which she could do well. To appear agitated wasn't difficult since she was. It would be difficult to then turn off the panic and pretend to be interested in getting drunk and having sex. She wasn't sure she could pull it off but had to try. She

129

would have to stay alert so she could look for car keys or shoes or a coat on her way out. And she had to be opportunistic to make it work. It would be hard to not think forward to what would happen when she escaped but she couldn't afford to look distracted when Adam came in. She tried to appear disturbed but was mentally trying to relax so she could do what she had to. She also had to look for any openings with Adam and be ready to exploit any chance that came along. Though she had never been a good liar, she had never been as motivated as she was today. Nora began to think outside of this room. She would call her father as soon as she could get to a phone so he could send reinforcements. Then if she didn't get very far before they found her, help would be on the way or they would have some idea of where to look. Maybe she should just try to find a phone and call for help. Surely they would be able to trace the call since she had no clue where she was. She could look out a window when she found one. Maybe there would be something she recognized outside and she would immediately know where she was. Nora was making herself crazier. She needed a plan so when she actually got out and was more panicked, she would still be able to act. She would make her way outside as quickly as possible and along the way look for a phone or peek out a window but getting away would be her first priority. She might not have much time depending on how consistently the room was monitored. Or maybe by that time the person watching will have lost interest since Adam would be in there with her, especially if they were sleeping.

It was just beginning to get dark when her plan finally started to work. She was beginning to think no one was watching, which was good and bad, when she heard the door being unlocked. She started breathing faster and her heart started racing. Nora was scared, but not of Adam. She was afraid of her plan but she was still convinced of its necessity. Adam slowly opened the door and looked at her oddly. She backed away from the door until she ran into the wall. Adam walked in and closed the door. She took a deep breath and steadied myself. He was reading her and she couldn't stand up to the scrutiny. She tried to convince herself she wouldn't do it. She would try to keep Adam with her, to sleep, but that would be it. She would make the decision whether to go later, if everything went okay.

That helped. She was able to look him in the eye and after a few minutes he stopped reading her face. She should have known she wouldn't be up to that level of trickery.

"Nora, what is going on?" he asked, looking at her suspiciously.

"I can't stand being alone anymore," she said, which was true. "I wait for someone to come in here all day and I'm not sure who it will be. I can't be alone any more or I will lose my mind."

"I just left you a few hours ago. And you slept most of that time. I saw you thinking about something furiously. What were you working on? Based on your expression then and now you are up to trouble. Please, Nora, don't try anything foolish. I'll stay with you as much as possible but I can't promise that I'll be able to stay the whole time. As a matter of fact I know I won't be able to stay here all the time. I have some other responsibilities and I'm trying to work things out for you," he said. Unlike her, his face was unreadable. She had to assume he was telling her what he thought she needed to hear to be a complacent captive. She would play along.

"I don't know what you are talking about. What could I possibly do? I'm stuck in here, all by myself. I just don't want to be alone. Can you at least spend the night with me? Please?" She asked, getting more upset and beginning to drip tears. It made her angry to cry but she couldn't help it. Everything she said was true. That would be her only chance with him. He would see through anything else.

"I'll stay as long as I can. Are you hungry?" he said, sounding more genial.

"Yes, I am. I haven't eaten since yesterday. You do realize that I've only been fed once a day since I've been here," she said. She was angry at her treatment. It was no wonder she was getting emotional. Adam could tell her anger was growing. He tried to diffuse things as quickly as possible.

"I'm going to order some dinner and get some wine and we'll spend some time together tonight. Okay?" He asked, trying to appease her.

"Sure. Could I take a shower while we wait for dinner? And you should bring two bottles of wine. I intend to get drunk tonight. Why shouldn't I? Maybe the time will pass faster if I am wasted," she said, a little bitterly. He just nodded and said he would be right back to take her to the shower. Okay. Things were progressing but she had to get him at least tipsy without getting herself too drunk. If he had some drinks then maybe he would fall asleep and not just wait for her to fall

131

asleep and leave.

She was worried about what would happen to him if she left. Would he get into trouble, or would he be killed? Just because he wasn't letting her go didn't mean she wanted him to die. He sure did pick a bad profession. Up to this point she thought jobs like bond trading were risky. She had no idea. There were many things that she would see differently if she made it through this. He was true to his word and returned in under ten minutes. After being blindfolded and led to the bathroom she showered and brushed her teeth. Adam watched, as usual. Being naked made her feel even more obvious. She tried to dismiss it. It only worked when she aborted the plan again. She wouldn't make a go decision until much later. It was just business as usual right now. She managed to get through it and didn't think Adam noticed. She felt his eyes on her and it made her blush. Hopefully he would assume she was flushed from the hot water. She didn't want things to go too far in that direction if she could help it. She needed to focus on getting him to drink with her. However, she did want him to stay interested. Maybe he would loosen up some if he were feeling friendly.

She dried off slowly and tried to decide how she should act but it was hard given her state of distraction. She was a practically crackling with anxiety. She knew everything could just fall apart. Nora took some deep breaths as he dried off her back. It helped steady her. He rubbed lotion into her shoulders and back as she stood in the warm and still steamy bathroom. His touch rubbed away most of the distraction. By the time he finished, she was taking deep breaths, lots of them. He gave her some clean clothes of the same type as before, a t-shirt and shorts, both oversized. No underclothes, again. And of course there were no shoes, not even socks. She'd think about that later. She sat on the bed while he went to get dinner. Adam wasn't gone long so he must have had someone else pick up dinner. He laid a sheet on the floor and set out plates and napkins. Then he lit a candle and poured two glasses of red wine. He continued to unload the picnic dinner of spaghetti, spinach, and bread. If she knew where it had come from she might have an idea of where they were. But there weren't any restaurant labels on the packages to give away the origin of the food. Everything was delicious. They ate, drank, and laughed. She relaxed, and then he did too.

Once again, it was hard to believe they were adversaries. It did no good to play 'what-if'. She never would have met him if not for this situation. Nora couldn't imagine him mixing in the normal Memphis social scene, although he would have done well. He was very handsome and charming. He would have had his pick of ladies willing to spend time with him. She could just see him at parties with the twenty-something's flirting and laughing at his wit. And it made her a little angry imagining it. She was beginning to feel possessive of him. It was madness! She was jealous of a fictitious scenario that she created in her mind, about a man who had kidnapped her. He had succeeded in making her crazy. She should just give up. Adam was watching her again, actually laughing at her.

"You're so funny. I would love to know what goes on in that pretty head. The emotions that cross your face are amazing. What are you getting yourself worked up about?" He asked. It didn't make her feel good to be so transparent. She had to get control of her mind, no matter how deranged it was.

"I would prefer not to discuss the craziness going on in my head. This place has done irreversible damage to me. I really don't want to be serious right now, but I want you to understand the seriousness of this situation," she answered soberly. He became serious too.

"I have never forgotten how serious this is. I'm trying to make things as pleasant as possible until it's over. I don't want you to get worked up about things you can't change. It not only won't help but it can do you much harm. I've told you that my responsibility for you is tenuous and dependent upon your submission to me. That's why I'm trying to keep you as calm as possible," he said. His speech made her angry but she didn't want him to know. If they argued it wouldn't accomplish her goal, and he might decide to leave.

"I understand what you're saying. It's hard for me to stay calm when I'm left alone so much. It makes me feel like I'm going crazy. My thoughts and fears spin out of control. I haven't given you any reason to think I'm not going to do everything you tell me. I want to live through this and trust you to get me out alive. I don't care about why you needed me, or what you know. I want to walk away from this and never look back. I've done it before and can do it again," she answered. He leaned toward her slightly and looked more alert. He refilled her glass of wine. It really was good. She felt warm and at least physically comfortable.

"Can you tell me about it? I'd like to hear what happened," he asked. Nora hadn't told anyone about what had happened during those two days she was held for ransom when she was eight. She'd never even considered doing so. Adam may be the only person she would ever be able to tell. He would understand on a level her parents never would. She had even been afraid to tell the psychologist. What did it matter now?

"I've never told anyone about what happened. I'm not sure the words will come out but I'd like to tell you. Maybe you'll tell me something about you? Maybe you will understand how much it means to me to leave this alive," she said, meeting his eyes. She took a steadying breath and started telling the tale. She'd replayed it so many times in her mind that it was there, but had been suppressed so completely the ready words felt awkward.

Nora described the party to him and how she thought she should've been allowed to go. She told him about sneaking out and finding the men in the garden. She told him about falling, and hurting her leg. The police would later find the blood that had been dripping from her wound. They were able to find smudges of it on the wall where she was roughly handed over. The images and fears came back to her like she had pushed play on a long paused movie.

As she was being shoved into the car, she called out and one of the men slapped her face and growled at her to be quiet. She had never been slapped before in her life. Shock and fear, as much as pain, made her cry. She was sure her dad would get her before they could drive off, but he didn't. It was the first time she could remember feeling that he wouldn't be able to help her. In her small world, her father had been all-powerful. Nora had complete faith that he could fix anything. That belief was shattered in the moment she was closed in the car and taken away. She remembered trying to make herself small in the backseat so they wouldn't notice her. She had stopped crying so she wouldn't make any noise. She prayed she would disappear. She was taken to a small house in a neighborhood with other small, dirty houses and yards with more dirt than grass. She was put in a chair against the wall in the living room and told not to move. The three men took off their jackets and sat around a table and looked at each other. Finally one of them spoke to her. He asked her what her name was and who her father and grandfather were. Nora told them. She was hoping that if she answered the questions politely, then she would get to go home. Her grandmother always said that please was a magic word so she used it. It wouldn't prove to be magical for her. She overheard many conversations she didn't understand and couldn't remember. She heard phone calls with her father and was even allowed to speak to him twice, but only long enough for her to beg him to get her. The men just laughed at that. They were mean. They would eat and not let her have any until they were through, and then only a little bit. They made her drink water from the dirty bathroom sink, and use the bathroom with the door open. She always held it as long as she could because she was so embarrassed. Night was the worst. The men drank liquor and even made her drink some. It burned her mouth and made her cough. She thought they had given her poison, because she couldn't breathe normally for a minute or two. This happened a few more times, and then they let her go sit down again. It was a good thing because the room started to spin just before she felt hot and sick. The man who spoke the most came over and sat beside her. All three were mean, but he was cruel. He would drop her food on the floor so she had to pick it up and brush it off to eat it or she would starve. If she cried, he would laugh. If she walked by him close enough for him to reach, he would pinch her. The cruel man was smiling at her, which made her afraid. He pulled her onto his lap, even though she was fighting him the whole time. Her elbow hit him in the nose while she was struggling to get free and he yelled, hit her, and dropped her on the floor. Nora lay stunned on the floor. She wasn't sure she could get up, and her stomach felt even sicker. The man walked around the room for a minute holding a tissue to his nose. The other two men didn't say anything at first but soon said things to the man that made him angrier. He would snap back at them and then glare at her. She knew she had to get away. She struggled to her feet and drunkenly ran towards the door. She hadn't made it halfway when his arm grabbed her around the waist. It was so tight she could barely breathe. He picked her up and carried her into a room she hadn't been in before. She kicked and screamed but his arm only tightened, and then she really couldn't breathe at all. She was starting to see black when he threw her down on an unmade bed with sheets that were stained and smelled like sweat. She coughed and tried to sit up. The men in the other room were

135

laughing. The cruel man was breathing heavily and taking off his shoes. He undid his belt and pulled it out of the loops slowly, staring at her the whole time. She didn't know what that look meant, but she knew it was very bad. Nora sprang up and ran toward the door but he reached out and slammed her back on the bed. He was laughing now, but not in a happy way, and it scared her more than when he was yelling. After slamming her down he put a leg over her legs and pinned her shoulder down with one of his hands. She couldn't move at all, no matter how hard she struggled. One of the other men walked to the door and when he saw what was happening he told the cruel man to stop, that she was just a kid. The cruel man yelled at him and told him to go away. The other man looked angry and said if he did it, he would be in trouble. She didn't know what he was talking about doing but she knew it wasn't good. The third man came to the door and agreed with the second man. The cruel man looked at them both and said that he wasn't going to really do it, just scare her. He looked a little weary of them, then firmly told them to go to the other room. They did. Her temporary relief was gone. He whispered to her that if she made a sound he would kill her. She knew he would. He put his hand on her stomach and then put his fingers under the waist of her panties, through her gown. She was terrified but too scared to scream. He released her shoulder, leaned over her, and lowered his face until their noses almost touched. She could feel and smell his hot, rancid breath. Her legs were still pinned and he was straddling her. In one quick motion, his lips attacked hers and he thrust his tongue into her mouth, filling it vilely. It was just enough to push her over the edge and she started vomiting. It came out of her mouth like a fountain, even through spurting through her nose. Vomit filled the cruel man's mouth, it being attached to her mouth, and he ran into the bathroom and vomited too. She continued to retch on the bed. The other two men were laughing uncontrollably. The cruel man returned as she finally stopped. When she saw the look on his face, Nora said she was sorry. He looked mad and sick. He walked over and picked up his belt off the floor, pushed her face down on the bed and started to hit her with the belt. The pain was so intense, with each stroke she thought she would die. He was on the third stroke before she could draw enough air in her lungs to scream in pain. She don't know how many times he hit her because each one felt worse than the one before. He finally stopped and left the room, with her lying on the bed full of puke, crying. She didn't know until years later that the beating was a blessing compared to what might have happened. She was afraid to go to sleep so she drifted in and out restlessly, curled up painfully in a corner of the room.

The next morning the men called her into the living room. They all looked tired and dirty. They told her to stand in front of them, turn around, and lift her nightgown. She did what she was told, too tired, hungry and in pain to fight. There was some arguing between them about the marks on her legs and back. She knew there were some on her bottom too because she felt them. But she wasn't going to offer to show them under her panties. One of the men was angry with the cruel man, saying she would have to stay another day because of the marks. The other man said it didn't matter. She promised not to tell anyone about what happened that night. Nora couldn't spend another night with them. After a few phone calls it was decided she would go home that evening if the ransom demands were met. It was a long day of degradation and fear of a repeat performance. They said that if her grandfather didn't do what they said, she would die. She prayed he would do whatever they wanted. She wasn't fed and was made to sit on the dirty floor where the occasional bug would crawl by, but she was okay as long as the men stayed away from her. She watched her captors carefully but her mind was far away from the dirty room she was in sitting in. She pretended to be in the garden at home or in her class at school or even at the beach, in the hotel, looking out at the waves crashing. Nora couldn't close her eyes though. She was so tired it was hard to stay awake. She kept telling herself that each minute that passed made her closer to going home. It was like Christmas Eve and waiting for Santa to come, or riding in the car on the way to Disney World. The waiting was too much to bear but each second that passed made it closer. She had heard her mother say that time marched on. She wished time would run. Late in the afternoon the phone rang. The call was to tell the men that the thing they wanted her grandfather to do couldn't be done until tomorrow. She would have to stay another night. The cruel man looked at her in a way that made her feel sick. She couldn't do that again. She was too tired and hungry to fight. She was already too hurt. How could she make it another night? She was trying not to panic, not to give them any reason to pay extra attention to her. Then she noticed they were looking at her. They had called her name and she hadn't noticed. Her father had asked to speak to her again. They held up the phone to her ear, and this time instead of begging for him to get her, she said one thing.

"Daddy, don't let him hurt me again!" she said, with unmistakable desperation. The phone was quickly taken from her. Her father was assured she was okay but wouldn't be for long if her grandfather didn't do as promised. They argued and finally the second man said that her father would get no more assurances. She was alive and if he wanted her to stay that way, her father would do as he was told and hope the terms didn't change. He hung up the phone quickly and cursed. The cruel man pushed her to the floor roughly and bent over to punch her when the second man stopped him. They fought and hit each other. She was afraid the cruel man would win, and then who would save her? The third man eventually stepped in and made them stop. She tried to be invisible in the corner. She knew the cruel man was still a danger to her and would be until she left.

Nora didn't cry or complain. She sat as still and quiet as she could and gave them no reason to think of her. She didn't ask for food or to use the bathroom. They would offer occasionally and she would accept, but that was it. The men decided to take turns staying up during the night. They were all drinking, but not as much as the night before. She was given a pill to swallow by the second man and choked it down without comment. It made her feel light, like a balloon floating off the floor and to the ceiling. She wasn't worried anymore, didn't even feel like she was in the dirty little house at all. She slept off and on, dreaming so much she wasn't sure what was dream and what was real. She dreamt the cruel man was smiling at her. He wasn't mean anymore and was holding her hand. She dreamt they were walking at the zoo and she was holding a balloon. It was windy and the balloon kept lifting her off the ground. She was afraid she might fly away like Winnie-the-Pooh, but the cruel man held on tightly to her and she didn't fly away. The dream went on for some time. She was sad and then scared of flying away and the man would pull her back to him, which scared her too. It was a very strange dream, which she didn't like to think about too much.

She was still sleeping the next morning when they loaded her into the car. She was happy to be going but couldn't stay awake. After riding for some time, she was still tired but able to open her eyes for more than a second or two. Then she realized she was about to be sent home. Nora was afraid to believe it but then they stopped on the side of the road. She didn't recognize anything. There were trees and bushes so thick the car almost looked hidden when they got out. She couldn't walk very well so the cruel man carried her. She hated being so close to him but tried to just think about going home. They went down a trail and around until popping out of the woods into a clearing where she could see her father's car. The cruel man set her down and pushed her toward the clearing. She was afraid to go at first. The cruel man bent over and quietly, malevolently said "I could keep you as my little girl. If you tell anyone about anything that happened I will come back and get you and make you mine. Run, or you'll stay with me." Nora ran as fast as her wobbly legs could take her. Daddy didn't see her until she had covered half of the distance. He ran to her, picked her up, dashed to the car, and drove them away as quickly as possible. She didn't even have her seatbelt on. She and her father were both crying. She would never forget how bad it felt to see him so upset. Over the next few days she was taken out of town, examined by doctors and talked to psychologists. She told them almost nothing about what happened. She wanted to forget about it and talking about it made her too sad. They kept prodding and asking, but it upset her so much her family stopped. She went to the psychologist's office for the next two years. She didn't remember telling her anything about the two days but they did talk and she drew many pictures. The psychologist seemed satisfied and Nora's family acquiesced to her wishes by not bringing it up at all. She knew they wanted her to talk about it. But she didn't want to see her parents upset again, and she was afraid the cruel man would come back for her if she did. So Nora never told anyone. Until Adam.

Adam had not said a word during the story and still seemed to be in thought. She was glad he hadn't stopped her because she didn't think she would have been able to finish. Nora felt relieved after finally sharing the nightmare with someone else. And while she briefly felt that old panic of the cruel man coming back for her and making her his little girl, she also felt free of it for the first time. She wasn't a little girl anymore. She could still be taken, and had been, but the old fears no longer held power over her. They had been replaced with new, very real ones. She waited for Adam to speak, not comfortable in the expanding silence. She was beginning to feel like it had been a mistake when he stopped working out whatever he was doing in his mind. He looked at her and his face softened.

"It was good for you to get that out. I think you did the right thing by not telling anyone else, but you needed to tell me. Did you know you remembered so much?" He asked, speaking softly and gently as if he were afraid of spooking her.

"No, it just all came out like it was connected by a rope. See, I can keep a secret. I wouldn't have told anyone at all but you're different. Somehow I feel like I have to tell you everything. How is that, when I have only known you for a few days?" She asked, truly dazed at the reality of the statement.

"We have an unusual bond. It has everything to do with the circumstances under which we've been together. I'd love to say it's because we are so good together but you know that isn't necessarily true. We'll never know how we would have felt about each other if we'd met in some other way. I'm happy we're together right now," he added, as if apologizing for bringing in the reality of the situation.

"Yes, I'm happy you're here too. I'd hate to think how things may have been without your protection," she said. He was beginning to feel bad for her. That was a dangerous place for him to be given the circumstances. Nora had been through more than any child should ever have to go through. Adam had abducted a few children in his line of work but had made sure that there was no terrorizing of the child, just the child's parents. Also, he would never tolerate a pedophile. If he saw that gleamed in any of the men he worked with, he disposed of them. He protected the child from the facts and reality of their captivity and tried to make it seem like a game. As far as he knew none were the worse for wear after their return. He knew he was rationalizing. He'd never heard about the experience from the child's point of view. Before now. "No more," he thought. He would not travel that road. He needed to focus on his current assignment. He had to manage Nora and try to get her through this alive if he could. She seemed at ease and docile but he knew she wasn't. He had seen fear and panic flash through her eyes a few times tonight and knew that something was going on. Adam decided wine would help her to calm down and maybe take away foolish inclinations toward executing any plans she may have. She was so easy to read. He held her glance and looked at her with a serious expression.

"Do you have something to tell me?" He asked. She squirmed a bit but regained control.

"No, I don't," she answered. She knew he suspected, and her chances of success had just dropped dramatically.

"Nora, try to trust me. I'm your best chance. If you do something risky, there will be no taking it back and the repercussions severe. Please think carefully," he said. She was thinking, and didn't want to go through with the plan, but couldn't see any real alternative. Adam might let her leave eventually, but maybe not. And especially after reliving her last captive experience and all the bad that happened, she wasn't willing to chance a repeat performance. Of course, she did get returned home that time.

Adam refilled her glass, again, and she gratefully drank it, enjoying the warmth it provided. She didn't want to think anymore. He changed the subject so quickly she wasn't even sure he had spoken the warning he gave her. She wouldn't have to respond or endure a lecture, but he'd made his point. She followed his lead and moved to a less controversial subject. She'd just shared the most traumatic event of her life and she knew nothing about him.

"Where do you live?" She asked boldly. "And what's your real first name?"

"Nora, you know I can't tell you. It would be a disadvantage for you to know…" he said. She interrupted him and said, "you tell me to trust you with my life, and you will tell me nothing about who you are. I don't want to know how to track you down. I just want to know something about you. Anything real and not just part of the role you're playing." She was beginning to plead, getting anxious again, when he stopped her. He knew she needed to hear something that would help her make a stronger bond.

"I'm from California. My parents have been dead for years. I have one brother. I have never been married or even close. I graduated from college. My job is my life now. I travel most of the time and have several peers but very few friends. I'm older than you are but I'm sure you knew that. Does that help?" He answered casually.

"Yes, a little. At least you're a real person now. When did your parents die?" She asked.

"When I was a teenager but I can't tell you any more than that," he

141

said. She seemed satisfied and moved to topic she was more curious about.

"Do you date? Have you had any significant relationships? How many other captives have you been sexually involved with?" She asked, but regretted the question as soon as it crossed her lips. She didn't really want to know. He didn't seem upset by the question. He knew women well enough to know they couldn't help asking but didn't want to hear the truth. His job was to understand the female psyche and exploit it as necessary. He could use one of the best manipulation tools there was, jealousy. She would keep her distance and not care about him too much, until she thought someone else might get him. Then she would have to have him. It worked every time.

"I date and have had a few relationships. I travel for my work so I don't have much time, but I do manage to fit in some fun. I've recently been seeing someone. She thinks I'm an international import/exporter. A relationship can only go so far based on lies. And I can't tell her what I do; I can't tell anyone what I do. It can be lonely," he said. She thought for a minute before responding.

"I already know what you do. Does that mean we have a chance outside of this place?" She said. What was she thinking? Was she really asking for a relationship with a mercenary, especially when she knew what he could do with any prisoner? He killed Allen, or at least had Allen killed.

"Are you asking me to be your boyfriend?" He asked, amused by how predictable she was. She was irate at his amusement and her stupidity.

"Of course not. I was just asking in theory. We've made the best of this and parts have been very fun but it doesn't change the fact that I'm not here willingly and you are being paid to be here," she said flippantly. She didn't want him to think she would be pining away for him when this was over. That was assuming she would be alive after this. Maybe she should give him some motivation to get her out of this alive.

"Are you interested in seeing me after this?" She asked hesitantly. She really did want to know.

"It might be possible. I could meet up with you for vacations, abroad of course, and we could have fun. You know I'll never be able to settle down and live a suburban lifestyle," he answered. She nodded in answer. Nora knew their reality. She just didn't want to stare it in the face right that moment. She had to respect his honesty even if she didn't like it. It would have been much easier for him to just tell her what she wanted to hear. They drank more and settled back against the wall on the bed and talked about fun places to meet for vacations. They laughed and highlighted the best and worst options. She could tell he'd travelled extensively and knew many of the countries better than a tourist ever would. She was more than a little buzzed and began to get tired. Adam seemed tired too. She asked him to stay and he said he thought he could. They undressed and slipped under the covers. Witty humor, relaxed conversation, anticipation of romantic vacations, and two bottles of wine were a perfect recipe for stoking passion.

Adam had wanted to take her in the shower, which was an example of just how screwed up this whole job was. He cared about her too much. He wanted her too much. She was beautiful, and sexy. But what tipped him over the line were her strength, her bravery, and her resilience. And after everything she'd been through, for her to have those qualities was a testament to her character. It didn't hurt that she looked at him with blatant sexual hunger. Well, after she'd stopped hating him. She couldn't hide her emotions at all. And he probably liked that about her best. In his world, everyone hid everything. And they were all very good at it. She was incapable of hiding anything from him. He could read her thoughts across her face like subtitles in a movie. He'd seen her make a plan then set it aside several times that evening. He intended to distract and exhaust her. He may not have known Nora Anderson for a long time, but there were parts of her he now knew well. She would be thinking of nothing except her next orgasm until he lost control. And he was very good at control.

She snuggled tightly to him, small spoon to his big. He folded his arm around her, pulling her against him more. She wiggled her hips, burrowing into him. As tired as they both were, it soon became obvious they weren't going to sleep. They each needed the comfort of the other too much. His hand ran from her hip to her breasts, possessively, as if taking stock and finding everything as it should be. His touch caused her hips to move again. She could feel him change against her, getting harder, more insistent. His hand reached between her legs and he felt for her warm cleft. He found her slippery and wet, ready for him. He smoothly slipped a finger into her core, causing her to gasp and move against his hand. His position made her body fully available to him, but she was frustratingly denied access to his. She turned her head toward him but before uttering a word he captured her mouth with his. She reached back, gripping his hip as an anchor during the onslaught of his passion. His mouth moved from her mouth to her neck, biting, kissing just as he removed his finger from her. Nora was frustratingly close to climax. Aching from lust and unable to take control from her position, she was suffering from her need and ready to complain as she felt his hardness pressing against her. She arched her back in response, inviting him in. He pushed through her slick opening, moving slowly and gently until she could accommodate for his size. His fullness caught her breath. His rhythm was slow but true, pulling almost completely out before burying himself completely. Nora was so ready that after only a few strokes she called out his name as her orgasm violently overtook her, squeezing him so hard he was almost ejected. There were no more gentle thrusts; he pounded into her, holding onto her hip and shoulder. His every movement only made her orgasm continue, drawing it out until her curled toes began to cramp. She didn't care. Adam finally came with a roar of pleasure mixed with triumph.

Neither moved as they continued to breathe heavily, still enjoying the afterglow of sex. Nothing seemed urgent in the peaceful haze. Snuggled together, still attached, warm and touching, anything was possible. Adam thought about where they were, what had happened. He had to stay grounded, and couldn't afford to indulge fantasy to himself. Though they had been tired, what started as a gentle, goodnight snuggle had quickly turned into focused ravaging, each knowing their time together was running out. He had to keep things separated in his mind. Distracting her was fine. Distracting himself, not so much.

Satisfied, well fed, drunk, and not alone, they both fell deeply asleep.

twenty-four

Sam trusted his men to protect Helen but he had to see her. He just had to actually look at one of his children. At the time it had seemed a good idea for Laura to be out of town but now he needed her support. Phone calls were not enough when his family was being snatched out from under him. Jeremy had reported that she was safe and settled. She wasn't happy about the arrangement but understood the necessity. Sam was careful to not be seen as he made his way to the condo where she was hidden. He went to the office first and changed cars before leaving the garage. He drove downtown, parked in the private underground garage, and rode up on the elevator. At that point he should have been greeted or challenged on the intercom by the team guarding Helen. When he entered the condo he did so with caution. Maybe the team wasn't in place yet, but Jeremy had reported they were. Sam called Jeremy, who answered on the second ring.

"I thought you said they were all set up? I'm standing at the door of the condo and no one has said a word or made a sound," he said. Jeremy was alarmed at once.

"Sam, I'm sending in a response team. Get out, now," he said, calling the emergency response director on another phone as he was speaking to Sam.

"Jeremy, I'm going in to get Helen. Get your people here as fast as you can. I'm not leaving my daughter," he said as he pocketed his phone and walked to the door. He opened it slowly and quietly. His best chance would be to sneak in and surprise them. Sam Anderson was no small man. At six feet two inches he was taller than average, but the years had added extra weight and inactivity had sapped most of his former strength. He would still be a worthy opponent since the prize would be his youngest daughter. Sam didn't have a weapon. Laura didn't like it and he hadn't felt like he needed to carry one for some time. Jeremy would have someone there shortly and would be there himself soon after. He knew he should wait but he couldn't take the chance. As he stepped in the living room he looked for anything out of place. He hadn't spent much time there but had been to the condo enough to know everything looked okay. He walked quickly under the loft to the stairs so he couldn't be seen from above. He still hadn't heard a sound. He started climbing the stairs carefully. He wouldn't be visible from the loft until he was about half way up. As soon as he could see, he scanned the upstairs for someone watching. No one. Then he heard a sound. No, it was more than a sound. It was more of a moan. It didn't sound like Helen but he couldn't be sure. He moved up the stairs more quickly. The first room had an open door and was empty. He moved to the second and opened the door. Nothing. He moved to the room he knew would be Helen's. He opened the door and looked in. He tried to take everything in and process it as quickly as he could. Two guards were standing beside the bed. They were looking at the door as if expecting him. There was another guard on the floor, unconscious. He couldn't see Helen. His anxious mind was trying to make sense of this when he heard the moaning again. It couldn't have come from the guard on the floor as he had yet to move. There must have been someone behind the bed or in the bathroom. The door just beyond the bed was open.

"What the hell is going on here? Where is Helen?" He asked.

"What are you doing here?" Asked a heavily accented man. Sam did not recognize either of the two men. He would have remembered that accent. He took two steps into the room looking for Helen.

"Tell me where Helen is. I'll give you anything you want, just give me back my girls," he said. He said this calmly. He didn't want to seem unreasonable. He would do whatever he had to do.

"Mr. Anderson, we know you will do whatever we ask. We have your daughters. What choice do you have? I wouldn't expect to see them any time soon," said the accented man. His accent was thick but his English was perfect. They were baiting Sam Anderson. They hadn't planned on taking him but since the opportunity had presented itself they decided to take advantage of it. He would be an easy target. Sam knew time was on his side since Jeremy and the team would be there any minute, but he couldn't wait. He took another few steps until he was well into the room and could look for Helen or signs of violence. He saw blood on the floor and some on the wall like someone had fallen against it bleeding. A lamp was on the floor and a pillow was across the room. The bedside drawer was partially open. His pulse was racing. He had to find Helen now. He started to round the bed when the guards stepped forward. Sam stopped. He knew he was outmanned. The two men kept walking toward him.

"Let me see Helen. Just let me see her, please," he asked. They ignored his request and each grabbed an arm. They had shuffled him out into the hall when they heard the alarm ding that someone had entered the garage. So they knew he was coming, Sam thought, and that would be his security. The men ducked back into the room and pushed him into the bathroom. One guard went in with him and one stood behind the bed as he had done when Sam came in. Maybe a moment or two later Sam could hear the team storm the condo. Sam looked around the bathroom to find a way out. He couldn't help his daughter if he were stuck in here. He could see another of his guards on the floor behind the door. This man was probably dead. He had blood all over him. Maybe the blood in the room was from him and not from Helen. He must have been the source of the moaning. There were no other doors and no windows from this room. The linen closet. This was a safe house and the room he was in was for the target or protected person. There was a secret escape hidden in the linen closet. He remembered it from when the condos were built but not any details. He would have to wing it. Maybe that's how Helen got out and why the guards were still there, looking for her. Hope began to swell in his chest. He walked toward the closet since his captor was listening at the door for the advancing team of security guards. Sam opened the door and looked in. He saw nothing strange. He pretended to be hiding when the guard looked his way. The guard sneered at him for his cowardice. Sam was able to search for the way out behind the partially closed door. He found it behind the robe hook. The shelves slid out of the way quickly and silently. He stepped through and pulled the door closed and locked. Then once he was on the other side from where the shelves he pulled the lever that made the shelves slide back into place. He could hear the guard beating on the door for a few seconds as it closed. He could only barely hear the gunshot as the man tried to shoot through the door.

Jeremy heard the gunfire and scrambled everyone to action. The silence had given them hope that maybe nothing was going on, or that maybe they would be able to negotiate. Now there was no denying it. The men pushed through the upstairs doors almost simultaneously and found the guard in Helen's bedroom. They shot him before he had his gun half up to firing level. As he dropped the other guard came out of the bathroom shooting. He was shot immediately. Both of the men were dead within seconds of each other. Jeremy ran into the bathroom and found the dead guard but no Sam. He tried the linen closet door. The locked door told him everything. He knew Sam must have gone through. He just hoped Helen had done the same. There had to be others who came with these two men. There was no way that they could have done this on their own. Jeremy started to make his way to another entrance into the secret passage to let Sam know it was all safe. No one would be able to get through the linen closet door until the system was reset. The door was reinforced with steel and there was no key for the lock. Jeremy knew where other entrance was, through the closet in the next bedroom. He hoped it would not be locked too. He could get in there but it would take a little time unless Sam reset it from inside and came out. On his way Jeremy called to one of the men and told him to go and look at the surveillance starting from the minute he left earlier that afternoon. He had to find out what happened and where everyone was. One of his men was dead and one was near death. He was stopped before he reached the next bedroom. An ambulance had just arrived along with the police. What a mess. He would have to explain three dead bodies, gunfire, an injury, and two missing people. This was going to be fun. He wished he were in the safe room with Sam. He would have to handle this first and then try to get in through the other entrance.

Sam followed the hall and went down a set of stairs until he was in a safe room. He really didn't want to be stuck in there so he continued to another way out. Helen couldn't afford to wait for Jeremy to get him out. He needed to find her. There was another hall opposite from the door he came in and he followed it. There was an escape route because being trapped in a safe room wasn't always the safest place to be. Sometimes you just had to get away. He followed the unlit hallway until he came to another door. The door was locked but he was able to find the release and it opened easily. The door opened into a part of the underground garage that he had never seen. A black SUV was sitting near the opening with the motor running. Sam ran to the SUV and opened the back driver side door. Helen was lying in the back seat, bound and partially conscious. One man was in the driver seat and another man was sitting on the back seat with Helen, on the passenger side. The man in the back casually looked up and smiled sardonically.

"Mr. Anderson, what a nice surprise. I didn't expect you. You must be the reason my men have been delayed. Since your security force is never far behind you I think it wise to leave," he said.

"You are not leaving with my daughter. I don't care about you or anything you want. Just give her to me and you can go free," Sam said.

"Yes, well, I will be going free and I will be taking her with me. She is the reason I came. Nothing else interests me," said the man in the back seat. Sam shook his head and reached in to get Helen. Where was Jeremy? He had to get here before they pulled away or he would never see her again. As soon as he grabbed Helen the man's arm shot out and caught Sam's arm, clinching it tightly. Sam cringed but didn't let go of Helen. He grabbed her around the waist with his other arm and tried to pull her free. He had the advantage because he was standing and could use his legs for leverage. The man in the back seat let go of Sam's arm and wrapped his arms around Helen, under her shoulders, and calmly told the driver to go. The SUV started to pull away slowly. Sam couldn't pull her away with the SUV rolling. She was literally ripped from his arms as the door began to close. He wouldn't let the car go without him. He couldn't let her get away. He held on to the door as it slowly went through the garage door. After it had cleared the garage it picked up speed. The driver turned onto the street and floored it. It flung Sam off of the door and into a police car parked in front of the condo entrance. The policeman standing outside ran to Sam and called for help on his radio. One of the security cars was outside too. He left Sam and followed the SUV. He knew his employer would want him to follow what must have been the abductors of his second child. Mr. Anderson's injuries were being treated. There would be nothing else he could do to help. He radioed Mr. Knight and told him what happened. Jeremy told him to stay with the SUV and not be noticed if possible. He was also to keep contact with Jeremy so that if he were seen and eliminated Jeremy would have an idea of where to go. Jeremy sent two other cars to catch up with him so there would be no chance of losing the SUV. There was a possibility it would lead them to Nora as well as Helen. Jeremy went out to the street to check on Sam. The ambulance was there, having already been dispatched with the first call for the police. The police at the scene performed CPR until the paramedics got to him. He was pronounced dead and left in place for the coroner. Jeremy rushed to his car. He would have to call Laura soon, but he hoped to be able to balance the bad news with the good, that he had found the girls. If he called her now he would have to tell her that both of her daughters had been kidnapped and her husband was dead. It was a phone call he would avoid at all costs.

twenty-five

Nora woke up suddenly, mostly because she had to go to the bathroom. As soon as she was alert she remembered what she was supposed to be doing. Adam was asleep in bed beside her. His breathing was deep and rhythmic. If she was going, it had to be now. She was afraid that someone might be watching. If she left and was caught her captivity would change dramatically. Adam would not trust her, and she might never see him again. What if the scary man took over? He would come back when he wanted anyway. She should go to the bathroom and see what happened. She could possibly talk her way out of serious trouble if she only went to the bathroom. Nora sat up very gently and crept to the door. She turned the handle gently, half expecting a siren to go off. It didn't. She knew the bathroom must be almost directly across the hall from her room based on her previous, blindfolded, trips. The hall was dark and cold but she could make out the outline of a door across the hall. She crossed the hall looking to see what was there. Darkness made it difficult to distinguish anything. First closing the bathroom door behind her, she turned on the light. She quickly relieved herself as she considered what to do next. No one was watching them tonight or she would already know about it. She knew she should try to get away, but she didn't want Adam to be killed because of her. And she had no doubt it was a real possibility. He had done plenty of things that would justify her wanting him to be punished, but he had also protected her from the other men. These last few days could have been much worse and she could be dead right now, but Adam had helped her. She couldn't do it to him. She would wake him up and try to get him to leave with her. Her father would give him plenty of money to get away. She turned off the light and opened the door. She crept back into the room and sat on the bed. Crawling over to him she put her arm on his shoulder, except it wasn't his shoulder. It was a pillow. She pulled back the covers and he wasn't there. Just as she started to back off the bed the lights came on. Her eyes closed in protest; she couldn't see anything for the span of a few seconds. When her eyes did work again she was facing the door and Adam was standing there in his jeans looking tired and mad.

151

"What were you doing?" He asked.

"I had to go to the bathroom and didn't want to wake you up," she said. Her answer was a little hesitant which made it sound less than credible.

"Interesting. Then why were you just trying to wake me up?"

"I didn't want you to get into trouble."

"By leaving the room you could have caused me trouble. Luckily we were not being watched tonight. You still haven't explained why you tried to wake me up if you only had to pee, and had already done it." Adam was getting angrier. She would have to confess and try to get him to go along with her plan. It would be a long shot but she would have to try.

"Adam, I'm going to tell you everything, just please listen to me. I was going to the bathroom, but I also wanted to see if anyone was watching tonight. When I was able to leave the room, I knew they weren't. I was going to escape, but I didn't want you to get into trouble because of me. I came back to wake you up and beg you to please come with me. We can go away someplace where no one will find us. I know you have the skill to do something like that. My father would give us any amount of money we needed..." She stopped because she realized she had been talking so fast and with such desperation that he probably wasn't following her. She looked at his face to see how much angrier he was. His face was blank. Maybe he was considering her offer. He saw the light of hope in her eyes and felt sorry for her.

"I have never met a more naïve person in my life. I'm glad no one was watching you escape tonight because it would have cost us both a lot. If you had escaped it could have meant both of our deaths. How far do you think you would have gotten? And I knew the minute you woke up. I just wanted to see what you were up to. I could afford to take the chance since I knew no one was watching. Nora, there is nowhere in the world to hide from this team. Maybe I could alone but not with you. And I don't want to go into deep hiding for the rest of my life. I intend to keep this job. Why would you think I would do this? I've never told you anything like that. I have always let you know how things were and that I would do my best to get you through this okay," he said. She didn't have anything to say. She couldn't argue with him. He had never promised her anything more than trying to help her and maybe a vacation in the future. She was glad she had come back to the room instead of his catching her trying to find her way out. At least he knew she hadn't double-crossed him. Her intentions toward him had been good. She hadn't lost him as a protector. It wasn't much but it was something.

"Adam, I'm sorry. I just wanted to do something to get out of this. I'm scared. I don't want to die here or remain a prisoner indefinitely. I want to have a life that's more than waiting to be fed or taken to the bathroom and left alone in between. I didn't mean to imply we would run away together like a couple in love. I just want to go and I don't want you to be in trouble. I guess I am naïve." She stopped trying to explain herself. She walked back over to the bed and lay down, staring at the ceiling. He would go and she would be alone again. She would try to sleep to make the time pass faster. She wished she had more wine to drink so she wouldn't care as much.

Adam continued to stand in the door, watching her. He could see the defeat in her eyes. It was something he had seen many times before but had never wanted to see it in her. He wouldn't leave her right now. In the morning he would, but not now. He turned off the light and walked back to bed. He slipped off his jeans and got under the covers beside her. She was surprised and rolled over to look at him.

"I thought you would leave," she said.

"No, not until morning. Please don't try that again. I don't want you to endure the pain of what would happen if you were caught," he said.

"Can you promise me that you will get me out of this alive? And preferably unhurt? If you promise me I will believe you and I won't try again. Otherwise I may not have a choice," she said.

"I promise. But you must be completely subservient to me. No matter what I tell you to do, and no matter who sees it. If you can do that and not let your pride or stubbornness control you, then I can get you through this. There is no other way. The others may test you, or make me test you. Just do what I say, and I'll be able to save you." Adam was getting worried. He wasn't sure she would be able to come through this. There were a few possibilities, all of which could fall through. But he was telling her the truth about needing to obey him and that the others might test her. He knew there was a pretty good chance she wouldn't make it but she definitely wouldn't if she tried to escape again. If Sid had been on the camera instead of getting Helen then she would be in his hands now. And Adam knew she wouldn't make it long with Sid. If Nora had to die, Adam would do it. He didn't want her to suffer for even a second. He would do it without making her afraid. It was all he could truly promise. But he couldn't tell her that. Nora wouldn't be able to wait for her death sentence. Adam hoped it wouldn't happen but he wasn't where this might end. The ultimate objective had not been made known, although his job was clear. Get and keep Nora Anderson. Don't let her be caught by the mayor's squad of tough guys and vice cops. Get her away from her boyfriend, 'Allen', before he killed her. He did that. Then he was supposed to find out what she knew about her dad's business and the kidnapping from her childhood. He did that. Now he was waiting for the next set of instructions. He hadn't been instructed to make demands for Nora's return. That didn't bode well for her. He would do what he could but had limitations. He would contact the client tomorrow morning and request more information. Then he would have a better idea of what he would have to do. If it looked bad he would drug her to keep her calm and oblivious. Then if he had to end it, she would never know. Sid would be back soon with Helen. He had to make sure that Sid didn't let Nora know. That would make his job impossible. Nora would stop at nothing to protect her sister and would get them both killed trying to save her. He needed to talk to Sid as soon as he got in. That would mean leaving Nora, which wasn't a great idea right now either. She was still upset and wouldn't be calm enough to sleep for a while. He would have to help her along tonight.

"Nora, I know you're anxious. I wish I could solve it all for you right now but you'll have to be patient for a bit longer. Would you like me to give you something? I wouldn't knock you out, just give you something to help you relax," he said. He hoped she would take it. He really needed to talk to Sid.

"Adam, I don't know. It's tempting. I'm just afraid. What if that man comes in again? I won't be able to defend myself." She really was tempted. It would be nice to drift away for a while and not think.

"Nora, I promise that man won't come near you. I'll stay in here with you or be close by. I won't go far enough for anything to happen to you." If Sid went for her, it wouldn't matter how alert she was. She would have no chance. But what Nora didn't know was that Sid would not be interested in her anymore. He had Helen. Sid would not be leaving Helen any time soon. She had injured his pride by getting away from him the first time he tried to get her. Adam felt sorry for Helen, but Nora would be as protected as she could be.

After a minute more of contemplation, Nora nodded her assent. It would be more controllable than alcohol and didn't include a hangover. He told her he would be back and retrieved the medicine. The drug Adam chose was something a little more of a sedative than he described but it was for her own protection and she wouldn't notice the degrees of drowsiness anyway. She took the pills without comment and snuggled into her pillow. He lay on the bed beside her, rubbing her back and playing with her hair. Her breathing became deeper as she was more relaxed. When he was sure the medicine was working and she was asleep, he left to find Sid.

twenty-six

Helen was barely aware of anything that had happened. She heard voices and tires squealing and maybe even her father's voice. Now she was coming out of the fog and knew she was riding in a car. She tried to look around to see where she was and who was driving. As she tried to sit up the car swung around and she was dumped onto the floor. She tried to get back up but couldn't until someone grabbed her arm and pulled her onto the seat. She looked toward the person helping her and saw a face she hoped she would never see again. Sid laughed at the terror in her eyes. She pulled away from him, he let go, and she fell back down. The adrenaline helped to clear her head as she attempted to get out of the car. She tried to open the door with her tied hands but he wrapped his arms around her and pulled her back toward him. He could have completely incapacitated her but enjoyed the struggle. The more she fought, the more he enjoyed it. This was so much better than her frozen sister. Nora had no fight in her. Helen was a wildcat. He was still angry she got away before but was all the more excited by the challenge. The driver was enjoying the struggle in the backseat too. He had taken them down empty streets to avoid anyone seeing the fight. It would take longer to get back but it was worth it. Sid had just ripped her blouse and her pink satin bra was winking at him. He watched as much as he dared because Sid didn't mind, but he would be in serious trouble if he wrecked the car.

The driver was much too distracted to notice the car following him from a discreet distance. Especially since that car had traded with a partner a few times. Jeremy was several blocks behind the primary car but was close enough to move in when he was needed. He kept in close contact with the cars by phone and had a team ready to move in as soon as they had a location. He expected there would be a messy fight and he would need everyone he could get. These were top of the line soldiers for hire and they had been two steps ahead of his security force the whole way. He owed it to Sam to get his daughters back. If he lost Sam and both of the girls his career would be over. He was having a difficult time anticipating where the SUV was heading based on the reports he was getting. The route seemed more random than planned. Jeremy wasn't sure what to do. The latest report was that there was some kind of struggle going on in the SUV. The details were sketchy but there was definitely something going on. The driver of the primary car was waiting for a decision of whether to close in or to let the SUV go on and follow it. Jeremy didn't want Helen hurt in any way, but he didn't want to miss the chance to get Nora back too. He knew if they stopped the SUV Nora would be gone for good.

"Just keep following but let me know what else happens," Jeremy said. He would hope Helen was okay and try to save Nora too. He knew that would be what Sam and Helen would want to happen.

Helen was confused and scared and hurt. She couldn't get away from this guy. She knew she should stop struggling but she couldn't make herself calm down. She was panicked. Sometimes when she pulled away he pulled her back and sometimes he shoved her more before helping her up. This along with the motion of the vehicle and the drugs made her disoriented. She had called for help from the man driving but there was no response. She gave up on him and continued to fight. After several minutes of struggling she finally sank to the floorboard and stayed there. The man seemed to be okay with that and left her there. She tried to think about what to do but her thoughts were still fuzzy. She couldn't remember what happened at the condo. She remembered getting there and lying down to take a nap but not much after that. She was certain she had heard her father's voice but didn't know when or how. She was afraid to look at the man in the backseat with her. She knew he was the same man who had hurt her before. She still had the bruises on her face from their last meeting. Things were different now. She was alone, drugged and this man had help. And he was probably mad at what she did to him a few days ago. She tried to gather her strength and courage as she waited for her head to clear. Sid was not fooled by her retreat to the floor. She may have had her head hanging down but he knew she would mount another attack and he couldn't wait. They would have fun tonight.

"Get us back. No more voyeurism for you. I'm ready to work with Miss Anderson, alone," Sid told the driver. He nodded and made his way back to the building where they had been working. Helen knew this would be the end of her. She couldn't be taken to this place or she wouldn't come out alive. She had no idea how much suffering could happen before the end. She would try to get away after they stopped.

It would do no good to struggle in the backseat anymore. She needed to be able to run and scream. She carefully worked on the restraints on her wrists. If she could get them loose she would have a better chance. Sid knew what she was trying to do and did nothing to stop her. He knew it wouldn't matter if she did get them off. He was ready for her this time.

twenty-seven

Laura knew something was wrong. She had not been able to get Sam on his cell phone for the last hour. She had tried to call Jeremy to let him know and he hadn't answered either. Jeremy's not answering was something that had never happened before. She called the house and the corporation and no one could tell her where Sam or Jeremy was. Laura tried not to panic but she felt like she was living her mother's nightmare. She and her mother had been at the beach. Just like all the times before, except that time she had her daughters there too. Daddy was supposed to come the next day but never made it. This was too much like before. She had talked to Sam a few hours ago. He'd said he was going to see Helen and then would call and let her know how Helen was doing. He should have called her back over an hour ago. He wouldn't tell her where Helen was because someone could have been listening to the phone lines. She was fine with that. Now she wouldn't even know where to look. She called the airline and booked a flight out the next morning. She would have gone immediately but there were no more flights and it was too late to even charter a flight from such a small airport. It had to be over soon. She couldn't shake the feeling that this was like losing daddy all over again. Nora had been gone then too. Why had her family been the target of so much violence? She had been afraid enough for two lifetimes. She would have to pull it together and be strong for the girls, and for Sam. He was a tough man but was very vulnerable where his daughters were concerned. He needed her right now. She went to walk on the beach to fight some of the anxiety. She carried her cell phone with her and prayed Sam would call. She had been walking for about thirty minutes when her phone rang. She didn't recognize the number but answered it anyway. The man on the phone wouldn't say who he was but he let her know what he wanted. She couldn't speak for the shock but listened intently. The man on the phone told her they had Nora and Helen, and that Sam was dead. It couldn't be true. This was what she was afraid had happened. The man on the phone wanted some files from Sam's office and money. She squeaked out an assent and memorized the instructions. She ran back to the house as quickly as she could and repeated them to the security guard there as she wrote them down. She told him about Sam being dead and Helen taken too. The guard was instantly on the phone with Jeremy and confirmed the news. Laura spoke to Jeremy for less than a minute, just long enough for him to tell her he was tracking Helen and might be heading to where Nora was being held. She let him go so he could focus on the girls. She didn't need Jeremy Knight to help her grieve for her husband. She called her mother and broke down. If anyone in this world could understand her pain it was her mother. After some time she thought about the ransom demands. If Jeremy weren't able to get her children tonight then she would give them whatever they wanted. Nothing mattered besides recovering and repairing what was left of her family. In the morning she would get on the plane and go home. Hopefully she would be able to hold her girls while they grieved for their father. If not she would go to Sam's office and get the files the kidnappers demanded. What they asked for didn't make much sense but she would find them and turn them over to get their daughters home. Then, after the girls were safe, she would bury her husband.

twenty-eight

The more research Lt. Whitman did the less he liked the connections. Nora was convinced the men chasing her were men he knew to work for the department. Those men were closely related to the mayor. Mr. Anderson had generously supported the mayor during all of his elections and his pet projects in between election years. If the vice cops had killed Dedrick Ray as Nora had said, then why? Why would the mayor want a kid like Dedrick dead? Lt. Whitman had watched the press conference where the mayor had condemned the killing and blamed the city council. No one would kill a child for political posturing. That was crazy. The case where Nora had been kidnapped before bothered him too. What had Sam Anderson done to get her back? He said the FBI had impeded her return. Anderson didn't mention his father-in-law had been murdered the day after her release. That should have been significant information. Whitman was beginning to see the edges of the picture but was far from solving the puzzle. He decided to look up the cases Judge Hunt had been hearing the two weeks before his death. The federal court dockets had been busy so it would take a while to research them all. He called in a favor and got two officers to assist him in the research. Whitman was looking into Anderson's holdings when the call came in from an officer downtown that Sam Anderson was dead. The officer gave a brief account of what Mr. Knight had told him and what he had seen. Whitman was already standing before the officer could finish the sentence.

"Hold Jeremy Knight until I get there," he said. The officer quickly jumped in with a response.

"Sir, he left already. He got a call and left," the officer said.

"Don't let anyone else leave until I get there. Do you understand?" Said Whitman.

"Yes sir."

What were they thinking downtown? How could they let Jeremy Knight leave when they had multiple dead bodies and no one else who seemed to have a clue what was going on? What a mess. Hopefully Mr. Knight would come back. Whitman called the corporation and left a message for Mr. Knight to call ASAP or to return to the crime scene, whichever he preferred. The sarcasm wasn't lost on the security guard on duty who also wondered why Mr. Knight would leave the scene. Now that Anderson was dead Whitman would be able to look at his financial records and maybe he would find the connection to all the pieces. When he had spoken to Anderson on the phone Whitman could tell he was desperate. If Anderson had confided in Whitman maybe this could have been avoided. A few clues would have been nice. Whitman believed Anderson truly didn't know who had Nora. The least he could do for the man now was to find his child.

twenty-nine

Nora was asleep and blissfully unaware of anything, but Adam looked in on her frequently. He was worried about her given what was happening. He'd just received a report from Sid's team and things didn't go well during their mission to get Helen. Sam was dead, which might be good for Helen and Nora. The pile of dead bodies at the scene was not good for them. His client would be displeased, as it didn't fit well with their low profile, discreet orders. Sid didn't seem at all worried. Adam suspected it was because he was anticipating his time with Helen. She had really gotten to him. Normally Sid could be depended on to keep things going smoothly and to be worried when things didn't. He seemed oblivious to the unraveling situation happening right now. Adam walked back into the room with Nora again. She was so peaceful. He was happy she was asleep because it would be hard for him to hide his stress from her. The last time he walked to the other end of the building Sid was getting Helen settled. Adam wanted to make sure Nora wouldn't be able to hear anything going on, especially Helen screaming. Knowing how it would affect Nora made Adam angry with Sid. He was surprised to realize the truth in that. He argued to himself that it was the lack of need that made him angry. With the death of Sam Anderson came the start of wrapping up the job. There was nothing to be gained by torturing Helen. Just feeding Sid's hunger for sadism. Adam had never flinched from it before but there had always been a clear agenda and expediency won out over compassion. That was not the case here. His orders were to get Helen and keep her until further notice. She didn't have any information they needed. Adam heard something and jumped from Nora's room and closed the door. The sounds were faint, from the distance, but unmistakably screams. Sid hadn't wasted any time. Adam was in a difficult spot. If he put a stop to it he would be burning a bridge with Sid. Sid was not someone you wanted as your enemy. If he didn't do something Nora's sister would be tortured and maybe killed, for nothing but a man's pleasure. Adam couldn't let that happen either. Adam had gone to the control room to watch Nora sleep and to keep a watch over Sid too. He could see in the room from the camera but couldn't hear anything, just like Nora's. It was hard to watch but he needed to make sure Sid didn't kill her. He would allow this for a short while then create a reason for Sid to have to leave. Adam was going over his options and keeping a close watch over Sid when he caught something in his periphery. He turned to the other set of cameras and studied them. There it was, cars, moving slowly toward the building. It was an old warehouse that had parts converted into a series of small rooms made to look like a house from the inside. The outside looked mostly abandoned. This had afforded them with extra security although it didn't do much good when you let them follow you here. Damn it, Sid. If he hadn't been so preoccupied with the girl this wouldn't have happened. After this Sid wouldn't be a problem again. You didn't get to make screw-ups like that twice. Adam could have sounded an alarm that would have alerted everyone about the approaching security force. It looked like the men in the cars were waiting on more guys and were grouping, so Adam had a bit of time. He thought for a second but knew he would do it despite the risks. He shut off the monitors and went to Nora's room. Nora was sound asleep and stayed that way even after he picked her up. He left the fabricated hallway and went down the stairs to a parked car. He gently put Nora in the passenger's seat and fastened her seat belt as she began to stir. He would be able to drive out the back access road without anyone seeing him. He drove quickly and was clear of the building before he made a call that made all the men in the building scramble.

thirty

Helen had loosened the bonds enough so that she could get her hands out. She kept them down like they were still tied until the vehicle stopped and the door was opened. As she climbed out she hit the driver with a closed fist and ran. She made it ten feet before the man from the backseat tackled her. She was slammed into the ground and the air was forced out of her lungs. Getting it back would be impossible since there was a man lying on her back. He took his time getting off of her so that when he did she shot up and gasped until her lungs filled again. She coughed and choked a few minutes more as the man laughed.

"How disappointingly predictable. Helen, I expected more from you. Did you think we would just let you run out of here?" He asked. She didn't respond. He was baiting her. She knew it hadn't been a great idea but she'd had to try something. He led her up the stairs and into a room with a bed, table, and nothing else but a carpeted floor. She hoped he would leave her alone in there for a while so she could think of a plan. He didn't intend to leave her for some time. He stood in the hall speaking to someone softly but she couldn't see who it was or hear what they were saying. She stood against the wall on the other side of the room. She stayed away from the bed. After much too short a time, he walked into the room and closed the door. He put his hands on his hips and faced her. She tried to stand up straighter and look him in the eye. She didn't want to cower in front of him.

"So brave, so proud. I will enjoy this. You won't of course, but I will," he said. She said nothing. She didn't want to provoke him, or encourage him depending on what he was looking for.

"I'll have to punish you for trying to run downstairs, and for hitting one of my men. You will learn the rules and I will have fun teaching you."

She was swaying a bit from the drugs but held herself upright. He took three steps forward and punched her in the face much the same as she had done to the driver, only many times harder. She fell hard to the ground. Her mouth was cut on the inside from her teeth. Blood filled her mouth and she swallowed it down, immediately regretting it. She spit the next mouthful out. He stood over her waiting for her to get up. She sat there, spitting out blood. After a minute he kicked her in the side. She yelled out and grabbed her side, lying down. He dropped to his knees beside her and pulled her hair back sharply so she was looking at him. She looked at him through the haze of pain. The only other time in her life she had been physically assaulted was by this man, a few days ago, and she still bore the marks from that attack. Sid pulled her face close to his and licked the blood off her lips. She quivered with revulsion but didn't try to pull away. To move would have meant pulling out some hair. She was very still and let him stay so close to her face that she could feel the heat of his breath on her eyes. He seemed satisfied and let her go with a shove. He paced around the room for a few minutes, trying to decide what he wanted to do first. Helen was terrified. She was afraid to do anything for fear of getting his attention and forcing him to act. Sid pulled her by the hair again, only this time it was to standing. She had her hands on top of his to prevent her hair from being pulled out. He led her to the bed and pushed her on it. Her shirt was ripped from the car ride and was gaping open. He told her to undress. She, of course, refused him just as he expected. Sid left the room and came back a moment later with a leather strap. He stood in front of her with it and told her to undress again. Helen knew he wouldn't hesitate to use it and began to take off her clothes, trying not to look at him. She had her clothes off but was still wearing her underclothes. Sid grinned at her and began swinging. The first assault landed across her thighs. She reflexively sat up to cover the pain so he hit her on the back next. Each time she moved to protect an injured part she exposed a new place for him to inflict pain. The blows landed so quickly she screamed repeatedly and tried to get away. He made no attempt to keep her in place. He just walked behind her swinging the strap. She couldn't get out of the room. After a few moments of this she had thick red whelps covering her body. She was cowered against the wall with her arms protecting her face and head, screaming. Sid stopped hitting her and waited for her to be quiet. After several minutes she calmed down as she noticed he was standing there, not doing anything. She knew it wasn't over and didn't want to guess at what might be coming next. Sid laid the strap on the table and told her to get on the bed again. She did so as quickly as her aching body would move. He pulled a knife out of his pocket and opened it.

The blade was four inches long. She screamed as he came at her with it but he didn't cut her, just her bra. Helen sat very still so she wouldn't be cut too. He then cut off her panties. He held the knife to her throat and she could barely breathe as he unbuttoned his pants. He pushed her knees apart with his knee and laid on her as she held still so he wouldn't cut her throat. As he thrust into her the pain was searing. She tried to separate herself from it, and the fear, just breathing in and out. Helen tried not to think about what he was doing to her, just to be still. Someone threw open the door and yelled for the man to come out. The man was furious but got off of her and left the room.

Helen was afraid to move. Was he coming back? Would he do it again? Should she move or would that make him hurt her more? In the end she didn't move until someone came in the room. It wasn't the man but Jeremy Knight from her father's office. He took off his jacket and covered her up while asking if she was okay. He knew she wasn't by the bruises, whelps and blood but she was alive and didn't look mortally wounded. He called for an ambulance and checked her heart rate. It was fast but strong.

"Helen, have you seen Nora?" He asked. She shook her head. She didn't trust her voice enough to tell him no. His men were searching the whole building but so far there was no sign of Nora. The ambulance arrived and Helen was put a stretcher. Knight walked out with her to see her safely inside. Before they closed the doors she asked if the men had been caught. Her voice was rough and raw from the screaming.

"We caught three men but there were more involved. We don't know yet how many got away," he said.

"Bring me pictures of the three you have. I want to know if the man who did this is still out there," she said without emotion. He agreed to do it as soon as he could arrange it. His guards questioned the three men until the police arrived. Jeremy Knight's interrogation technique was considerably more liberal than the police department allowed. He got nothing from the men. The police didn't question their condition when they took over custody. Jeremy called Laura and updated her. Laura would be on a flight in a few hours to take care of the ransom demands for Nora. She only hoped they would still be satisfied with the previous demands since they had been attacked by her husband's men, and three of their men were in custody.

Jeremy called the hospital and talked to the doctor treating Helen. She had two fractured ribs, bruises, cuts, and abrasions but she would be okay. The police had taken pictures and gathered evidence so they would be able to convict. She was being held overnight for observation since she had so many injuries. They had given her pain medicine and she was asleep. Jeremy had two men stationed outside her room to make sure the bastard didn't come back for her again. He wouldn't be able to get the pictures to her until the next day so he wasn't sure they had the man responsible for her condition.

thirty-one

Lt. Whitman was just wrapping up his meeting with the FBI. They had been very interested in the things he'd found out. They were able to make some connections Whitman hadn't been able to figure out. They had an open file on the mayor already but not enough hard evidence to convict. It was only a matter of time but they wouldn't show their cards until the case was ironclad. Whitman had been doing his research discreetly but evidently not enough so. After leaving the FBI office he was paged by his office. He was ordered to the mayor's office. It was a long drive from the FBI office in east Memphis to the mayor's office downtown. Whitman had plenty of time to decide how to play it. He wasn't really afraid for his life today. Even the mayor wasn't that stupid. His whole office, no doubt, knew of the summons and there would be much speculation as to the reason. Whitman showed his badge at the door and was allowed to carry his weapon in with him. He had to wait for fifteen minutes before the mayor would see him. So much for 'get down here immediately'. He had hoped to get it over with quickly. Finally he was called in.

"Whitman, what is this I am hearing about you? Are you checking up on me?" He asked. He didn't get the answer he expected.

"Yes, sir."

"Do you think that's prudent given my position?"

"No, sir. Not really," Whitman answered.

"Why would you do such a foolish thing? Surely you realize there is nothing to gain by it," said the mayor.

"While working my case I found out some very disturbing things about you and some of your family members, including one who works for the police department. I'm sure you know to whom I'm referring."

"Again, why would you take such a risk, and for what reward? You would only be feeding my opposition, which could result in upheaval for the city. Who benefits from this? I have the city's best interest at heart. These things you say you discovered are lies, lies created by my opposition. I am a threat to those who wish the city harm," he said, settling in to a political speech. Whitman had no desire to listen to the mayor's rhetoric.

169

"Sir, I have discovered more than rumors and lies. Your daughter-in-law killed a man with her reckless driving. You had a police captain jeopardize his career and falsify the report. You have also been appointing people to positions they had no business being in. That's nothing new for you, but I found out that they are manipulating anything within their scope to benefit you and discredit the city council." The mayor was standing up.

"That is enough. How dare you come into my office and speak to me so disrespectfully."

"With all due respect, how dare you mistreat the office of mayor? The people elected you and trusted you to lead with integrity, not abuse their trust for your personal agenda." Whitman knew this was counter productive. Fighting with the mayor was a bad idea on every level. He tacked to another direction.

"Sir, I don't mean to argue with you. I assume you are aware of what has been happening with the Anderson's. I know Mr. Anderson has been a long time supporter. After his daughter was missing I had no choice but to follow what ever lead I could find. It was she who sent me in your direction, indirectly. She recognized your nephew as the shooter of Dedrick Ray. I thought she was crazy..." The mayor sat down.

"She is if she said he did it. Why would you believe such a thing from her about one of your own?" He asked. Whitman didn't like that corrupt cop being classified as one of his own. He and men like him tarnished the reputation of the many great and honorable men and women who made up the police force.

"I dismissed it entirely, until I found out about the first time she was abducted. That in and of itself wasn't much until it was paired with the case her grandfather had been presiding over and his untimely death. The more I looked, the more connections I found, with you and corrupt police. After that, she didn't sound quite so crazy," said Whitman. The mayor had his hands in front of him, making a tent with his fingers, as he considered Whitman's statement. Whitman took his silence to be an invitation to continue.

"I had most of it figured out but not everything made sense. Then, after Sam died, I was able to look at his business and records closely. Laura Anderson wanted answers and gave me documents I never would have found on my own. Sam was holding interesting stuff about you, even way back. He must have researched you too," said Whitman. The mayor sat quietly as Whitman described to him things he never wanted anyone to discover, especially not an above board cop. Whitman explained his involvement in Nora Anderson's first abduction. Eighteen years ago the mayor held another political position without quite as much influence. He was, however, already manipulating things to play out for his benefit. He had more than one police officer willing to take direction from him for financial incentive. One such officer had been caught and indicted. The officer was promised freedom for his silence. Other officers used three criminals beholden to them to lean on the assistant district attorney for the charges to be dropped. That was what they were doing at a party at Sam Anderson's house on the night Nora sneaked out of her room. The men took her and the police officers helped the ADA to have a fatal car accident the next day. The men had threatened the ADA's daughter so he had not told anyone of the encounter. They used Nora as leverage to get Judge Hunt to find for the officer. After the Judge did it he was killed. Sam knew about that but not the mayor's involvement. Sam had supported the mayor through donations and support for many years but had recently been unhappy with some of the decisions the mayor had been making. A police captain had covered up the mayor's daughter-in-law's role in a car accident, which resulted in a man's death. She had been driving recklessly and caused the accident but the captain falsified the reports and named the dead man as responsible. The mayor had also made a series of appointments to positions that the people were not close to being qualified to fill. While such things were not new, they seemed especially blatant and were hurting the city by further dividing an already divided people. Sam had mentioned his concerns to the mayor and was not impressed by the mayor's explanations and threatened to pull his support. This had concerned the mayor because if Sam pulled out many would follow. He decided to hire Allen to date Nora and stay close to the family. He would be ready to take Nora if necessary to keep Sam's support. Then Sam had issued the ultimatum that the mayor turn in the police captain and admit his daughter-in-law's role in the accident. The shooting at Paulette's was planned by the mayor to scare Sam and Laura but had no idea that Nora would see the vice cop who shot Dedrick Ray. After that unforeseen problem Allen was supposed to kill Nora a few days later, assuming

171

things had died down. Instead things ramped up when an unidentified team blocked Allen and took Nora before he could kill her. The mayor didn't confirm or deny any of Whitman's report. He had a very smug look on his face.

"Very interesting story lieutenant. I doubt anything will come of it. After all, who would believe you over me," he said.

"Well, actually the FBI was very interested in not only the story but also the files and evidence." Now it was Whitman who looked smug and the mayor looked quite pale despite his dark skin tone. In truth, Whitman didn't know if the FBI would be able to put together a strong enough case to attack the powerhouse mayor but he enjoyed the thought of the mayor losing sleep, wondering when the indictment might come down. It was the least he could do for Sam.

thirty-two

Adam drove around while Nora was waking up. He knew the team would be coming for him soon. They would be able to find him because he would call them. The only chance he had in surviving this was to play as if it were part of the exit plan. But he had to pick a place that would protect Nora too. If they took her, she would be killed to tie up the loose ends neatly. Adam couldn't let that happen. This was Sid's fault. If he hadn't become obsessed with Nora's sister, which made him reckless, they would never have been found. It was the first time they had ever been infiltrated. Sid would have a huge chip on his shoulder and would be looking to put the focus on someone else. Adam fit that role perfectly. Nora became more alert and noticed they were in a car. Adam handed her clothes and told her to get dress as quickly as she could. She could hear the undercurrent of urgency in his voice and fought her way through the fog to do as he said. After she had changed clothes he gave her shoes. It felt strange to have on underclothes and shoes again. She sat up straight and tried to focus on the road. She didn't recognize where she was. It was surreal being out in the world again. She was almost overloaded with all the lights and words and fast moving cars. She tried to look straight ahead so she wouldn't get carsick. She thought whatever sedative he gave her must have been strong.

"What happened?" She asked. She had been nearly silent up to that point, sensing he needed to concentrate.

"Your father's security team found the building and were coming in. I had to get you out of there," he said.

"Why? Are you going to kill me? I thought you said you would help me," she said, getting more upset by the second as she realized what that meant.

"Calm down. If the team knew we were being breached they would kill you. I saw your dad's men coming and could have warned the team sooner but chose to get you out instead. Because of my decision some of my men were probably captured. If anyone knew this, or even suspected it, I would be killed. I'm trying to keep my word to you and deliver you home alive." She felt foolish for accusing him when he had maybe sacrificed his life to save her.

"Thank you." It was all she could say. She was worried about him. She had to help him get away.

"I'm taking you some place public so they won't be able to take you when they come for me," he said. She was outraged.

"What do you mean when they come for you? You aren't going to let them find you?" She said.

"No, I'm going to call them and tell them where I am," he said. She was incredulous.

"What are you talking about? Are you crazy? You're not calling them," she said.

"Nora, I know you don't understand but trust me when I tell you this is the only way I have a chance to live. I have to take the gamble and convince them I'm still true to our protocol and that my objective was our mission," he said. She tried to stay calm but her instincts told her to run away and for him to not get near those men ever again. She knew had to trust him. He hadn't let her down so far.

"Okay Adam, if you're sure then I'll do whatever you say. I just don't want you to get hurt because of me."

"I know. I'm not committing suicide, just taking a calculated risk. Actually a long shot, but I think I can pull it off. Just do exactly what I say and please don't argue. My plan has no room for variance or hesitation. I don't have much time to explain but I want you to know that I didn't kill Allen," he said. She gasped thinking of him after so much time of repressing it. She didn't really miss him that much only felt guilty about moving on.

"But he is dead. Nora, don't waste a minute feeling bad about Allen. That isn't even his real name. He was hired to watch you and then, later, to kill you. Only I intercepted you first." She found it hard to believe. Why?

"Who hired Allen? Who hired you?" She asked.

"Allen was hired by the mayor. I was not. I can't tell you the name of the person, only that he represents an old, very wealthy family in Memphis who were concerned about the city and the corruption of the mayor."

"What in the hell does that have to do with me?" She asked.

"Sam was a significant contributor to the mayor so they needed to know how involved he was and how much you remembered from the last time you were kidnapped. They also wanted to know more about the mayor's actions and enough proof to get him out of office. They considered themselves to be doing a public service for the city of Memphis," he said.

"All of this, the murder and kidnapping, my life, for politics? I can't believe it." She didn't have any idea how bad it was. She didn't know her father was dead and Helen was, well, Helen was half-dead, mentally, if not physically. Not many people could take much of Sid without permanent damage. He knew he couldn't tell her any of that or she would never be able to execute the plan.

"Come on honey, I need you to leave all that behind right now. We're not out of the woods yet. You have to follow my instructions to get away, alive," he said. She knew it would be nearly impossible but she would do what he asked, no matter what. She was very quiet as he called the team and told them where he was going.

Tunica County was the poorest county in the state of MS, and one of the poorest in the nation, before gambling was legalized there in the early 1990's. But once gaming became legal, casinos began popping up like weeds along the riverfront. The area flourished under the new revenue and became one of the largest gaming areas in the U.S. The collection of casinos commonly known to locals as "Tunica" was an hour south of Memphis, basically in the middle of nowhere. The grandiosity of the lights seemed absurd in contrast to the desolate darkness of the Mississippi delta. But walking through the doors of any of the larger than life buildings was to transport one right out of Mississippi. No longer were they in a rural, semi-impoverished land rife with social inequity. They were now in a fantasyland complete with bright lights, musical sounds, free drinks, sumptuous foods, and plentiful smoke. And to make the fantasyland complete, there was always the possibility of becoming rich. Winning money was a strong attractant. Even just the chance of it could make someone ignore the wizard obviously standing behind the curtain. This made Tunica an ideal place for the exchange. There was enough security to prevent anyone from acting aggressively. And as long as no one's behavior was overtly odd, or as long as they didn't put a coin in a slot and hit the big one, the people there would never pay a moment's attention to them. The biggest downside was the imperial presence of cameras. Every space on the casino floor was recorded. So blending and camouflage would be vital, along with no direct exposure.

Adam chose one of the biggest, and busiest casinos on the strip, The Horseshoe. It boasted having the loosest slots and biggest payouts, but that's what they all said. This one must have had something because the parking lot was full. Adam stopped at the end of an aisle and turned off the car.

"This isn't a spot. You'll get towed," she said.

"I don't care. I'm not leaving in this car. And neither are you," he said.

"Oh. Then I guess it doesn't matter. Is this the last time I'll see you? Is this it?" She asked.

"No. I told you, we'll get together sometime. Just don't worry about it now. You need to stay focused. I'm trying to keep you alive, and me too," he said.

"Yes, of course. Are you sure this is a good idea? We could still just leave. We should just leave," she said.

"No. Not an option. Let's go. Just like we talked about," he said as he got out of the car. She had no choice but to follow, each step feeling like a walk to the gallows. But she wasn't sure if it was to his death or her own.

The night air was crisp with wind gusts that were downright nippy. Nora didn't complain when Adam passed her a scarf and instructed her to pop up her jacket collar. She gladly did that and buttoned up. Adam had done the same and put on a ball cap, pulled down low over his eyes. He didn't look afraid, but his actions demonstrated how things had changed. He wasn't in control. He wasn't full of swagger and confidence. He had to blend and be cautious. He might not survive this. And he put himself in this position to save her. She wasn't sure how she felt about that.

They were greeted at the door by a smiling security guard. He welcomed them and even held open the door. If he had any idea of the trouble they were inviting into his area of responsibility he would have slammed the door in their faces. But to him and anyone else who happened to look their way, they were just a couple rushing in out of the cold for a night of entertainment and gambling. Adam steered her away from the gaming tables and cashier boxes. They headed toward the buffet and theater areas, strolling, like they were trying to find a good place to stop and give away their money.

"Should we play for a minute? Just a slot machine, to make it look like we a here legitimately?" She asked.

"No," he said. "What if you won? You can't walk away without it looking crazy suspicious. And it would draw too much attention to us. I know the odds are against winning, but it would be just your luck to hit it big the one time we need you to lose," he said.

"It's not worth risking it," she agreed. "What's the plan then?"

"My team will be here in two hours. Let's get a room," he said, smiling at her. They continued to casually walk through the casino to the hotel desk. Adam walked up to the receptionist and smiled charmingly.

"We need a room, please," he said.

"Do you have a reservation?" She asked.

"No, we just came down from Memphis to eat and gamble, but decided we wanted to drink and stay later so we'd better get a room. Do you have one with a king-sized bed?" He asked, leering at me openly. The receptionist probably assumed he'd already been drinking with the way he was acting. It was strange to see Adam acting like a normal person, in a normal situation, even if he was being a little embarrassing.

"Sure, we have a room available," she said. As they worked out the details Nora realized in less than two hours he would be gone. This was maybe the last time she would ever see him. He said they could vacation together, but would they really? He was an international mercenary. She was his prisoner. How screwed up was she that she even wanted to meet up again? She was an assignment. Sex may have just been a means to an end for him. He may have sex with all his "assignments". All that may be true, but Nora felt she could read something more than just lust in his eyes. There was plenty of lust too, but also something more. Her instincts had kept her alive this long, she decided to continue to listen to them, for at least two more hours.

The room was dark and cool, nicely decorated. It would be a good place to avoid attention and have some privacy. Adam put out the do not disturb sign and locked the door. She took off the scarf.

"If you want a drink from the mini bar you can have one. I need to keep a clear head," he said.

"No, that's okay. I don't need a drink. I'm just now getting over the pills you gave me," she said, trying to be light. The atmosphere in the room was tense. Maybe it was the wrong thing to say.

"I thought it would help you. You seemed to be so panicked," he said, a little defensively.

"I know. It did help. Thank you," she said, trying to smooth things over. Wow, what a weird place to be, trying to reassure your captor he did the right thing in drugging you. Several minutes of silence passed. Nora sat on the couch as Adam checked his phone. He read and sent messages. She went to the restroom. She closed the door without thinking, and realized she was alone. This was the first time he had allowed her to do that. She used the toilet, then washed her hands, all the while expecting him to walk in. The door was unlocked. He didn't come in. She used the complimentary toothbrush and paste left on the counter. He still didn't come in. When she walked out he was sitting on the bed with his shoes off, watching the flat screen TV. It seemed very normal. She paused for a second, not sure whether to join him on the bed or go back to the couch. He turned away from the TV and looked at her. He would let her chose. She kicked off her shoes and climbed on the bed. He clicked off the TV.

"I wasn't sure you were coming out of the bathroom," he said.

"I wasn't sure you weren't coming in to get me," she said.

"Did you want me to?" He asked.

"No, but you haven't let me be alone in the bathroom since we met"

"True. You learn a lot about someone by observing her most personal, private moments. And it's a great intimidator," he said. He wasn't bragging or conciliatory. He just stated the facts, as he knew them.

"If we're going to try to get together after this, and have anything at all, you are going to have to make peace with what happened and my part in it. If you can't, that's fine. I understand. If you want to try, I do too. But we can't tiptoe around what happened or pretend it didn't happen, or worse, rewrite what did happen. Do you think you can do it?" He asked. He was right.

"Honestly, I'm not sure. But I do want to try. I think I can get past it. There was some pretty bad stuff, but most of the time you kept me safe. I feel closer to you than anyone else in my life," she said.

"Okay. Just let me know if you change your mind," he said.

"How will I be able to reach you? Can I call you?" She asked.

"Not for a while. My team will probably lay low for a couple of months. Then I'll get in touch with you. We'll work out a trip and then a way to communicate. You and your family will need a few months to get over this. And if, during that time, you decide you can't get past what happened, I'll understand," he said. He turned toward her and smoothed her hair out of her face. She looked up at him, into his eyes.

"Months. That's a long time. I don't want to wait that long," she said.

"I know. I don't either. But that's what is best and safest for us both," he said. "Let's make the most of this time, okay?" He was right, again. She would mourn his loss after he was gone. Right now she could do everything she would dream of doing later. Nora pressed her lips to his. The kiss started sweetly, but grew to a starving, animalistic thing. Their frenzied movements succeeded in getting their clothes off, and then Adam slowed the tempo slightly by moving down and covering her with his mouth. Nora had no reservations this time. No one was watching them. As he licked and sucked, her pleasure built like a storm rolling into town. As he swept his tongue over her it was like the winds picking up speed. Each time he reached up, pinched and rolled one of her nipples, it was like lightning cracking across the sky. Nora was carried away by this storm of passion until Adam thrust into her wet core. She was adrift until her orgasm finally broke free like torrents of rain.

When their breathing became normal again, Nora realized she had tears on her face. She wiped them but not before Adam saw her.

"What's wrong?" He asked, softly.

"I don't know. I don't think anything is, really. I'm just overwhelmed. I've never had sex like this. It's never been this amazing. I'm a little in awe of it, and sad to lose it," she said.

"I understand. It is amazing. I don't want to lose it either. But you've had a crazy week. You may not know it now, but you need this time. What an incredible reunion we'll have," he said. Nora knew he was right, logically. But it didn't feel right, emotionally.

thirty-three

They showered and put back on their same clothes. Adam had his hat back on and pulled down low. Nora had the scarf back on. She held his hand and followed him, eyes down in a subservient way, just like he said. Every few minutes he would tug on her arm just enough to make it look like he was controlling her, but not enough to catch the attention of the guards. He knew at some point the surveillance footage would be reviewed. He wanted it to look like Nora was his captive, not his date. It would be easier for her that way. They would understand some degree of subservience and even her defending him, but only if he continued to act as they expected. If they looked like a couple then there might be doubts as to whether or not she was involved from the start. It would be much easier for the police to explain than his team's perfect extraction. Of course, when Nora found out the whole truth she would not be very likely to defend him, would she.

thirty-four

Jeremy returned one daughter to Laura Anderson. That wasn't good enough. Laura intended to give the files and money as ransom to get Nora back too. She would give anything to have both her daughters. Helen was in bad shape. Laura prayed Nora was fairing better but it didn't matter as long as they came home. They could spend the rest of their lives getting over this if only given the chance. Jeremy didn't think she should pay the ransom. He thought they should trick the abductors and just rescue Nora. Laura made it perfectly clear who was in charge and what they would do. After all, she told him, he already had the chance to rescue Nora but didn't. No more chances would be taken with her child's life, not over some money and files. Jeremy had warned her about Sam's files and the danger of their contents being made public. Laura made it very simple. Nothing else mattered but her girls. Sam was gone. Nothing would bring him back. Nothing about him or his business, or anything mattered. Jeremy would give the kidnappers what they wanted, where they wanted it and bring Nora back. Jeremy finally agreed. She didn't care what dirty laundry might fall out of those files. Her girls were all that mattered.

thirty-five

Laura had received a text message on her cell phone for the money and files to be delivered to The Horseshoe Casino in Tunica. How did those bastards even get her private number? At least she had agreed to let Jeremy make the delivery. There was no way he could let her go. Jeremy tried, unsuccessfully, to dissuade Laura from giving Sam's files to those mercenaries. He had quickly learned Laura would not veer from the course she thought led to Nora. Jeremy respected that strength and determination, even if he disagreed with what she was doing.

Jeremy walked into the bright lights of the casino carrying a thin briefcase and Laura's cell phone. When she acknowledged the meeting she told them she would be sending a representative. They insisted she come, alone. But they soon learned, as Jeremy did, that Laura Anderson was much tougher than she looked. She told them she was sending the files, the amount of money they asked for, plus ten percent more, and who was bringing it. She told them they had better give Nora back. She would be waiting, with Helen. They agreed. He assumed they weren't sure if she was stupid or crazy, but there wasn't much to do about either except work around it. So they did. Jeremy still didn't understand what was going on. After everything that happened, it turned out to be a kidnapping for ransom? And not that much ransom. Laura would have paid much more than that. The files were sensitive, but now that Sam was dead, not as valuable. The police had three of the team members, but they weren't saying anything. They all had expensive lawyers. Helen saw pictures of the men in custody, but couldn't positively identify any of them. She said one of them may have been driving the SUV when she was taken from the safe house, but she was still groggy and never saw him well enough to be sure. None of them was the monster who attacked her. Jeremy didn't call the police to let them know about the ransom. The police had problems in their own house and Jeremy didn't need any additional complications. He intended to get Nora back, no matter what.

thirty-six

Adam led Nora to a crowd, clustered around a craps table. Everyone was trying to watch the next roll, either cheering wildly or groaning, depending on how the dice bounced. Nora tried to peek at the table, assuming that was why they had stopped. Adam used the crowd as a cover to watch Jeremy Knight as he walked across the casino floor toward Jack Binion's Steak House. He continued to watch through the ups and downs of the craps crowd. Luckily for him, it was mostly ups, which kept the group intact. No one wanted to leave and change the luck or miss out on the payoff. No one was following Mr. Knight. No police had come in, before or after him. Good. Adam's team was already in place. He needed to make the switch without Nora getting hurt, or Mr. Knight seeing Sid. He wasn't sure if Helen had been able to give a description, but he didn't want to take that chance. Mr. Knight would be feeling bad about Sam's death and Helen's condition. He couldn't be trusted to maintain control if given the opportunity to extract vengeance from Sid. Sid deserved it, but Adam couldn't allow it. He already had three men sitting in jail, a situation he could have prevented and they all suspected it. He was going to have to walk a very fine line with these men as it was. He couldn't go against Sid right now. Adam was the boss, but he only had authority over these men because it was in their best interest to follow him. If he couldn't be trusted, they would not only cease to follow, but possibly stage a violent coup. He had valuable list of clients and a reputation. His team could decide to take it. None of his men would suspect he had real feelings for Nora. This was what he did. His brand of persuasion worked for most of their female captives. The only variation was getting her out before calling his men. And he would blame that on Sid. He could spin this, no problem. Then they would get their men out of jail. As soon as bond was set, they would hop on a plane and disappear. The client had already paid them for their services. The confirmation of the wire transfer was sent to him over an hour ago. The files and money from Laura Anderson were to confuse the whole situation and provide a bonus for his team. Money does help smooth out hard feelings. The last hurtle to completion of this mess was getting Nora safely home in exchange for the briefcase. This was really for the benefit of his men and Mr. Knight. They needed this for closure. Adam could have dropped Nora off at home and skipped on the briefcase, but sometimes giving people what they expect, good or bad, is the best way to satisfy them.

thirty-seven

Jeremy had been seated at his table for several minutes before getting a text to order three glasses of wine. He flagged down his server and did it. He tried to look relaxed, natural as he waited. The briefcase was on the floor, in between his ankles. He casually looked around for anyone watching him. The restaurant was packed. If he hadn't had a reservation waiting for him he never would have made it in the door. He knew from past experience the food was great, but eating was not on his mind now. The sommelier brought three glasses of red wine. He paused until he had Jeremy's attention.

"Where is the case?" He asked softly, in an accented voice. It took a moment for his words to register in Jeremy's brain.

"Under the table," Jeremy answered, looking carefully at the man now. It wasn't the man Helen described.

"Give it to me," he said.

"Where is Nora?"

"Walking this way. Hand it to me and she'll join you," he said as he motioned toward the door. His gesture looked to anyone watching like he was telling Jeremy his friends had just arrived. Jeremy looked toward the door and saw her walking behind a large man. He bent down slowly, grabbed the briefcase, and handed it to the accented man. Adam and Nora joined Jeremy at the table as the sommelier walked away with the case.

"Nicely done," Jeremy said.

"Thank you, Mr. Knight. That means a lot coming from you," Adam said, sarcastically.

"Nora, are you okay?" Jeremy asked, ignoring Adam's remark.

"Yes, I'm fine," she said quietly. She looked like she might cry but Jeremy didn't press. She had been through quite an ordeal, and she did look much better than Helen. At least this jerk had kept the sadist away from her. But it was probably only because he wanted her for himself. He had to stop thinking down this road or he would do something that might jeopardize Nora's release.

"Let's have a toast, to a deal completed," Adam said, as he lifted his glass. Nora lifted hers and waited for Jeremy. He paused for a second then lifted his too. They all tapped lightly, and then drank.

"Can we go now? Your guys have had plenty of time to count the money and check the files," Jeremy said. Adam looked at Nora, then down at his phone.

"Just another minute or two," Adam said. "Let's just drink our wine and have conversation, like everyone else." Nora picked up her glass and drank.

thirty-eight

Leaving Adam was bad enough, but having to pretend in front of Jeremy Knight was too much. If this weren't over soon she would start crying and cause the scene Adam was trying to avoid. Adam was drinking and baiting Jeremy. Those two were getting more hostile by the minute. She didn't understand why Adam just didn't leave. The server came by so Adam ordered an appetizer. Nora wanted to scream. Surely they weren't going to stay long enough to eat? Then she started to feel a bit dizzy. Maybe she should eat if she was going to drink. When did she eat last? Tipsy was okay under these circumstances. She had just about finished her glass of wine. One glass of wine couldn't do any real damage, she thought, as she reached for the glass. But instead of the wine she picked up the water glass.

Adam looked at his phone again. Sid was getting anxious to leave. Adam couldn't respond without tipping off Mr. Knight. Sid had better follow orders and not show his face or there would be hell to pay. Just another few minutes and it would be safe to go.

"Mr. Knight, please make sure there is an appropriate escort before you leave with Miss Anderson. Discipline has been an issue on this job and I haven't had a chance to address it yet," said Adam.

"Of course, but why concern yourself? You have everything you want," Jeremy said.

"Not everything," answered Adam, looking at Nora. Her eyes met his for just a second before he checked his phone again. Nora saw passion, and pain? She recognized the passion. Was she projecting the pain? He was a professional. He handled women like her for a living. He was still handling her. She knew she was such a fool to believe anything else, but she did. Her face felt hot, then all of her felt warm. How could she let him leave? Her thoughts became fuzzier as her body continued to heat up. Then she was so tired she could barely keep her eyes open. Adam was typing on his phone while saying something to Jeremy Knight. She couldn't even follow his words but could tell Jeremy was alarmed and angry. Adam stood up and casually walked away. Nora tried to say something, but her mouth wouldn't work. She had been fighting so hard to stay awake and struggling to speak, but

187

with Adam gone there no longer seemed any point. Nora laid her head on the table and faded to black.

thirty-nine

Nora woke in the hospital with her mother holding her hand. After several tries her eyes finally stayed open.

"Mom. Where's Dad?" she finally said. Laura Anderson hugged her daughter, tears running down her face. Within the hour the police and FBI had her statement, such as it was. Nora told them everything, except about having sex with Adam. That had been consensual, therefore none of their business. Jeremy came by her room after they left. He apologized for any mistakes he made during the situation. He looked broken, something she never expected to see in Jeremy Knight. Nora had been told about her father's death and Helen's torture. She was trying to sort all the pieces of grief without choking on them. Every time she added the Adam piece and thought of how he could have saved her father or stopped Sid she began to drown in it. She had to quickly cut those thoughts off before they overwhelmed her. Her eyes dripped a slow, steady stream of tears.

Everyone assumed it was the stress of being taken and the emotional release of being let go. And all that was true. But they didn't know that she was also grieving for Adam who she was sure was dead, while feeling guilty about caring for him at all. Her family was torn apart and would never completely heal because her father would never be there again. Nora didn't know if Adam could have saved Sam. What really bothered her was not knowing if Adam would have saved Sam.

The hospital kept her overnight so she could get IV fluids and have some tests done. Her mother was very happy to have her back safely, but it was a bittersweet reunion. Nora's father was dead and Helen was a mess in every sense of the word. No one could look at her without cringing. Helen stayed on strong painkillers for the first two days and then began to resurface. After four days she was released from the hospital but was still taking medication and seeing a therapist three days a week. Laura had the funeral held until Helen was released from the hospital. She knew Helen would have enough to overcome without missing her father's funeral.

forty

Nora stayed at her parent's house for a week to help her mother and Helen. She was glad to be with them during the aftermath but now she needed some time to herself. She was devastated by her father's death, but also by Adam's potential death. That grief she had to hide. No one would understand and she was having a hard time keeping it secret. Nora decided it was time to go back to work. Laura and Helen asked her to wait a little longer and go through counseling. Nora was afraid if she did her grief for Adam would come out. No, she wasn't ready to talk about any of it and maybe never would be.

Her first day back started fine. She was busy and had no time to think about anything but her job. Everyone was busy until around eleven. Then as the other nurses and nursing assistants began to get caught up they came by to tell her how sorry they were. It was kind but it was just enough to push her over the edge. After that, the memories flooded back into her brain and she couldn't make them stop. Maybe her mother and Helen were right. Nora couldn't stay focused but did her best and made it to the end of her shift. On her way out she stopped at her nursing supervisor's office and told her she was taking a leave of absence. Her supervisor asked her to please reconsider because it would make the schedule short but Nora had to refuse. She couldn't safely take care of anyone in this state.

She went home in a state of severe depression. Pulling up to her house brought back memories of her vulnerability and the death of her neighbor. She went in the house and locked the door a little too quickly. She walked into the dining room and looked at the table she had hidden under. She had to stop. Pushing on the bruise would not make it heal any faster, only make it hurt worse. Helen was doing better and Laura wanted to plan a ski trip for the three of them in Colorado. It would be a while before the beach would be appealing again. Nora called her mother and told her about taking the leave of absence. She would be able to go with them to Colorado so Laura should move forward with her plans. A change of scenery would do her some good.

Nora took off her uniform and put on some clothes for working in the yard. She thought that maybe a bit of work in the flowerbeds would be a distraction. And if nothing else, it would make her tired. She didn't really think it would work but she didn't have anything else to do that wouldn't make her remember. She had just tied her shoes when the doorbell rang. She was startled and panicked for a second, then pulled it together and answered the door, thinking she had to stop freaking out. It was Fed Ex to deliver an envelope. She signed for it and thanked the courier. Inside there was a note saying "meet me if you can" and was unsigned. Her heart skipped a beat as she realized what that meant. Adam must still be alive. She was flooded with such relief it drowned out much of the depression. She felt hope again. Also in the envelope was a first class ticket to Morocco, leaving the next day. She called her mother and only told her that she was taking a little trip but would be back in time to go skiing with them. She started packing carefully, making sure she took everything she needed. The last time they'd been together she had been a mess. She intended to make a better showing this time.

forty-one

He was looking at his computer screen, tracking the Fed Ex package. He periodically hit the refresh button until he saw what he was waiting for. Recipient signed for package. Sid leaned back in his chair and smiled as he planned their vacation.